Falling for Grace

A Coastal Hearts Novella

Janet W. Ferguson

This book is a work of fiction and any resemblance to persons, living or dead, or places, events or locales is purely coincidental. The characters are the product of the author's imagination and used fictitiously.

Copyright © 2018 Janet W. Ferguson

Southern Sun Press LLC

Southern
Sun Press

ISBN-10: 0-9992485-3-7
ISBN-13: 978-0-9992485-3-9

Acknowledgments

My thanks go out to:

The Lord who steadies me through the hard places of life.

My husband, Bruce, for supporting me.

My fabulous ACFW critique partners, proofreaders, friends, and my street team.

Editor Robin Patchen, mentor author Misty Beller, adorable models and friends Paige and Tyler Slay, photographer Ann Marie McGee, and cover artist Carpe Librum Book Design.

Forget the former things; do not dwell on the past. See, I am doing a new thing!

Dear Reader

This story deals with the incredibly painful grief of losing a child. I know I'm not able to adequately deliver the message of what horror that must be, having never lost a baby whom I had held in my arms. I did lose one through miscarriage, which was an extremely sad time for me—that deep ache of loss and disappointment. In my grief, I often felt isolated, since my husband and I were the only ones who had known this child—other than God. During that experience, I often mourned silently at the sight of fully pregnant women and infants born around when mine would've been, or reaching those sweet milestones. Not that I didn't want others to be joyful and have healthy children, but I wondered what my child would've been like, and those what ifs often spun through my heart. What if I'd done something differently? Had I lifted something too heavy, worked too hard weeding the flower bed? Was it my fault? I experienced the fear and worry of trying to have another child. Knowing in my heart, even if I did, another child was not a replacement for the baby I'd lost.

Losing a child goes against the natural order of things, breaking pieces of parents' hearts that can't be mended back to the way they were before. But I believe our God can take our sorrows and our tears, capture them, and form those crumbled shards in a new way, though painful, into something precious. We also need each other, friends. Grief support can be another way to climb out of that hollow, broken place. I pray for each of you

5

who might be grieving and want to offer those dashed hopes the promise of the One who binds up the brokenhearted.

In Him,

Janet W. Ferguson

Chapter 1

It was finally over.

Like some kind of cruel joke, mile after mile of long rays of Florida sunlight splashed across the steering wheel of the Toyota Camry, highlighting Grace Logan's empty ring finger.

Though her divorce had been finalized more than a year ago, and the separation had begun a year before that, she'd clung to a scrap of denial. As if what had taken place in her life had merely been an awful dream.

But in reality, Trevor had left. Claimed he wasn't happy, and he didn't love her anymore.

That announcement had ripped her in half—made her feel that she'd failed as a wife. The wound of rejection was still mending two years later.

Of course, the truth had eventually become obvious. Alexa had been the deciding factor. Apparently, Grace's best friend was able to make Trevor happy. Her friend succeeded where Grace had failed.

They'd married last weekend, and the betrayal had plunged Grace into an abyss.

She'd held her emotions together…until she'd seen the social media pictures post. The photos of the couple, smiling and hanging all over each other in the Caribbean, displaying their new bands of gold, bands that represented how they'd promised to be faithful until death parted them. The images twisted Grace's insides into an impossible knot, unleashed a new depth of grief over the loss of her marriage.

Vows were a covenant. Grace had taken them seriously. Hadn't she done more than her part to honor her commitment?

Grace attempted to hold in her tears, but her traitorous lip quivered for the millionth time that week. Christmas time had been difficult since her divorce. Amazing how fast things came around when you dreaded them. Not that she didn't love her family, but she couldn't take another year of holiday turkey served with a side of sympathy. This trip to Santa Rosa offered her a sanctuary before the state legislature convened in January. Time to pray through some of her negative emotions. When her boss suggested working remotely to prepare the upcoming season's reports—even loaning her the family beach house— Grace had taken her up on the opportunity. Brooklyn Barlow, the head of Roundtree Group and top lobbyist in Georgia, had lived through difficult times and had become a great support through Grace's personal disaster.

Grace slowed to scan beyond the pampas grass and wax myrtles lining the road. Her navigator announced the destination was near, but every three or four feet, another palm tree blocked her view. She squinted, attempting to better read the mailboxes or any address signs on the ornate wrought iron fences that outlined the beachfront properties. At last, she spotted the house number on an intricate metal gate in front of a brick driveway. She turned, stopped the car, and punched in an access code. The arms of the gate rose and allowed her entrance.

Pulling inside, she took in the crème-colored two-story mansion. This stately house boasted French doors upstairs and down with decks overlooking a pool on one side and the Gulf of Mexico on the other. Beautiful, but she'd expected no less from Brooklyn. Once she'd pressed a remote to open the garage, she parked and let her head rest on the steering wheel. Her breathing came in shallow puffs, so she inhaled deeply through her nose, held in the oxygen a moment, and then released it. She could get through this.

God, please help me get through this.

With shaking hands, she opened the car door and stepped out. Her flip-flops caught on each other, and she hurtled forward, barely catching herself on the Camry.

"Close call." She expelled a relieved sigh. The fact that she'd been named Grace had become something of a joke to her friends and family…and coworkers and random strangers who'd witnessed her multiple acts of klutziness.

No harm done. So far. Her suitcase lay across the backseat with her computer case. She grabbed them both and cautiously lugged them up the stoop. A serious fall here alone would be a catastrophe. She imagined the pathetic scene. Desperate and alone, she'd lie on the ground with a broken leg, calling for help. No one to hear. Flailing and bellowing like a beached manatee.

Stop it, crazy-head. That was not going to happen.

She never got seriously hurt. Not physically. And she'd keep her phone with her at all times, just in case.

She pressed another code on a wall keypad and then opened the door. A white chandelier hung above a massive abstract painting with blues and pinks and yellows merging together to resemble a shoreline.

A beachy scent enveloped her, soothing her frazzled spirit. How did that happen inside a house just because of its location? Too bad she couldn't bottle the aroma and take it home. If she had a home… She'd ended up renting a friend's extra bedroom way longer than she'd planned. At first, she'd thought surely Trevor only needed time. He'd change his mind.

9

At some point she'd realized intellectually that they were finished, but starting over in a new place required a lot of time and emotional energy. The high prices of real estate in Atlanta, along with a busy position, didn't leave a lot of either to spare. She'd have to make finding her own place a high priority after the session ended this spring. No more dwelling on the past.

With slow and deliberate steps, she climbed the staircase to the second level, where Brooklyn had said the master bedroom was located. Stairs had never been her friend. Falling up them, though seemingly impossible, had become her unintentional custom around the Georgia State Capitol, earning her quite the reputation with the representatives. The Speaker of the House had even given her an honorary certificate on the floor, *Most Falls without a Lawsuit*. Brooklyn had loved the attention the silly award brought, claiming Grace had endeared herself to the entire body without a word. Just a few bruises.

The bedroom materialized behind the first door at the top, and she dropped her bags just inside. More coastal-style oil paintings adorned three pale yellow walls, and a massive king-sized bed centered the other. A plush white comforter and pillows covered the mattress, a color a klutz would never invest in. This place was gorgeous. Hopefully she'd be able to keep it that way. She'd like to look at the rest of the rooms, but touring the house could wait. What she really wanted at this moment was to feel warm sand beneath her feet and sun on her skin. Though today was the first of December, the temperatures flirted with the mid-seventies.

The clear blue skies called to her. *Come to the beach.*

She slipped off her jeans and pulled on her one-piece bathing suit. Not as many worries about her waistline since twenty pounds had disappeared within the first few months

10

after Trevor's announcement. Wasn't hard to diet when food's appeal dwindled. She slathered sunscreen on the exposed skin.

All she needed was a towel, her phone, her beach hat, and maybe a novel—if she could concentrate.

Five minutes later, she shuffled across the boardwalk leading to the beach. An orange-and-black butterfly flitted by, carried on the breeze with the clear water and sky as a backdrop. How amazing. No one had set up camp around this little area of shore, so she'd have some peace and quiet. Just the sound of the surf and seagulls. Perfect.

Grace's foot dropped lower than she'd expected at the end of the walkway, and she toppled to the sand and rolled onto her side. "Oops." She hadn't been watching for the end of the decking. But another great thing about the beach was it made a softer landing place.

"Hey, are you okay?" a male voice called on the breeze.

She glanced around but her wide-brimmed hat had shifted, interfering with her view and leaving her no clue where the voice had come from.

"I'm fine." On the outside, anyway.

She gathered herself and made her way close to the surf, spread the towel and lay down. A light, salty breeze tickled her face. It rattled across her ears, toyed with the edges of her floppy beach hat. A faint buzz lifted her gaze skyward. Two propeller planes from the airbase drew white lines of exhaust as they crossed in front of her, their structure a mixture of airplane and helicopter. Brooklyn had called them Ospreys, told her locals said they were the *sound of freedom*. Then the planes disappeared, and the soft rhythm of the ocean took over. The white powdered sand and clear water rivaled the Caribbean.

Ah. Her anxious spirit unwound. She let her eyes close,

11

hoping her muscles would relax and the gentle waves would wash away the emotions harassing her.

A scream ripped the air.

Letting out her own scream, she jerked up and swiveled toward the row of majestic homes facing the sea. "Does someone need help?" she called.

To the right of Brooklyn's house, a flash of movement caught Grace's eye. She squinted to focus in the bright light. A man in a backwards baseball cap clomped across the next-door neighbor's deck and ran in her direction down the boardwalk. Wavy caramel brown hair poked out from the edges of the cap. Faded jeans fit his trim form, and the blue T-shirt he wore clung over broad shoulders. Nice. The short sleeves allowed the ripple of a bicep to peek out, too. She should really stop gawking. Where was he running? Was someone drowning nearby?

The man seemed to be aiming at her. "Were you hurt after all?"

"Me?" Grace glanced around to check if the man was speaking to someone else, but the closest group of people was at least three houses down.

"Didn't you holler for help?" His work boots dug into the sand as he came near and squatted beside her. Light blue eyes bored into hers. "Did you hit your head on a board?"

"Is there a bruise on my face?" She felt around her forehead for a knot or sore spot she'd forgotten.

"You seem out of it." His voice was silky and caring. A warm voice, if there was such a thing.

"I was enjoying the peace and quiet, then some loud noise scared the life out of me."

A hearty laugh shook the man's whole body. "My saw? That's what this is about?"

"A saw? I thought an animal might be dying."

"A wee bit dramatic, aren't we?"

What? "You're the one who ran down here like a lifeguard on Bay Watch." An extremely cute lifeguard on Baywatch.

~~~

Something about her made him smile.

Navy eyes stared out from under the lady's crumpled hat. The pale skies behind her only punctuated the depth of her deeper tone. The color couldn't be any bluer, like the dark hue of the American flag. Smile lines crinkled the corners of her eyes, though her expression remained serious. A smattering of honey-brown freckles, the same shade as her hair, dotted her perky nose. He resisted the urge to straighten the floppy hat. He should introduce himself instead of grinning like his cousin's performing poodle. "My name's Seth. I'm working on a few noisy projects out on that deck." He pointed toward the neighboring house.

"I'm Grace."

He quirked a brow before he could stop himself.

"Don't. Even. I've heard that joke my entire life."

"You mean it's a perpetual condition?"

"Apparently." She raised her elbow. "Got the scars to prove it."

He had a momentary vision of this adorable woman falling off the boardwalk. Only this time he was there to catch her.

Weird. When did he start having out-of-body experiences? He'd been alone for three years, and this kind of crazy reaction had never happened before. The warmth flooding him sent his fingers to scratch at the crew neck of his T-shirt.

"Thank you for your concern. I didn't mean to interrupt your work." She seemed to be dismissing him. "I'll know to expect a lot of racket coming from next door."

13

"You're staying at the Barlows' house? Are y'all related?" He hadn't noticed her pull up, and she didn't look like any of Brooklyn's usual crew.

"She's my boss." Her shoulders slumped, and Grace seemed to shrink a little. The posture incongruous with the smile lines that softened her face. "She loaned me the house for a while."

More protective instincts kicked in, along with some curiosity. "You're from Atlanta, then? That's where I'm from." Though he hadn't been back in a while now.

Her head bobbed, and her lip might've quivered.

Oh, not a crying woman. His gut twisted. How that tore him up inside, especially when there was no way to make things better. He'd love to tuck tail and run, but a nudge in his spirit held him in place. "Are you sure you're okay?"

She nodded again and offered a forced smile. "Long day. Long story. Thanks for the concern."

"You're welcome. I…I'll see you later." He took two side steps before turning away. His work boots sank into the sand, and he trudged back toward the house, his radar for pain sounding an alarm. Like looking in a mirror, he knew heartache when he spotted it.

Chapter 2

The hammer pounded the wood instead of the nail between Seth's fingers—the third time he'd missed his mark since his bizarre foray down to the beach. Was clumsiness contagious? The corners of his mouth tugged. Of course not. But his haphazard hammering had everything to do with the cute, navy-eyed woman. Grace. She had him distracted in a big way. Her eyes had been engaging enough, but she'd also had that slight quiver in her lip.

Seth laid aside his tools. Concern still niggled in his mind, and he could no longer ignore the prodding in his spirit to act. There had to be something difficult going on with Grace. He grabbed his cell and punched Brooklyn Barlow's contact.

"Hey, Seth. Did you meet my assistant already? Is she okay?" This powerful woman's voice held an edge of worry.

"That's what I'm calling to ask you."

A sigh traveled across the connection. "You know from experience how hard divorce is. Grace's situation was different than yours, but her husband marrying the other woman this week reopened a lot of rawness."

Divorce. Even now the word felt ugly. Like a name branded on him, although his own split was not a result of infidelity. Deceit at the level Grace had gone through had to have been terribly tough.

His own breakup had come because of a different sort of tragedy, and the soul crushing despair had sent him crawling to his family's beach home to regroup. Three years later, he was

15

still here.

"I'll keep an eye on Grace, if you want."

An uncharacteristic chuckle rumbled through the line. "That's exactly what I was hoping. I'm sure you'll think of a way to console her."

After he ended the conversation, Seth paced the house. The timing of Grace's appearance couldn't be a coincidence. Lately, his prayers had led him to believe he should stop playing the hermit and try to reach out to others in pain. Not to mention the fact that his parents and siblings had been bugging the stew out of him to pick himself up and start a new life. Of course, they'd love for him to come home and work in the Atlanta office again. He still managed their online accounts remotely, but recently his dreams had veered to opening a small, specialty branch of their hardware chain down in Santa Rosa, starting over here.

Grace's quivering chin returned to his mind. She'd been holding back tears, and not because she'd fallen in the sand. Maybe her arrival was some kind of sign.

His chest burned with the vision of her as if a blowtorch had seared his conscience.

The answer was as clear as the sparkling waves washing up in the Santa Rosa sun. He had to do something to help Grace.

Friends always told him he was quite the grill master. Seemed it was time to dust off the spatula. He'd get cleaned up and head to the butcher shop and seafood market. Nothing beat surf and turf. A nice grilled filet and Gulf shrimp delivery might perk Grace up. And give him the opportunity to offer a listening ear. Unless she didn't eat meat. He'd throw in a salad, too, and hope there weren't any tears involved. The sound of a woman crying was like a crowbar ripping away the walls covering his boarded-up grief. Selina's relentless tears, the sound of mourning and loss.

Seth closed his eyes. *God, if this is what You want, I'm relying on You to lead me.*

~~~

Grace poked a splotch on her forearm. The crimson skin faded white for a second before turning to red again. That stung. The bathing suit strap on her shoulder didn't feel too great either. She'd missed a few spots with the sunscreen. Somehow, she'd managed to get a sunburn in December, though she'd only been out a few hours.

Surely Brooklyn had aloe vera in the house. Grace trudged up the boardwalk onto the deck and rinsed the sand off her legs in the outdoor shower. A whiff of something delicious traveled on the breeze, and her stomach rumbled. The scrumptious barbeque aroma could tempt even a woman wallowing in self-pity. Too bad she hadn't gone to the market yet. There was a grill beside Brooklyn's pool. Once she cleaned up, she'd figure out the location of the grocery store and make her own steak. She could take care of herself. That was her life.

Alone. Unwanted. Betrayed.

No.

God was with her. The enemy wouldn't steal that truth. She'd squash those dark, whispered lies from the adversary.

God was her beloved, and she was His. Her joy had always been found in Him, and she couldn't let her circumstances hijack her faith.

The back door stuck when she pushed against it, and she dropped her beach bag just inside. She stepped onto the hardwood floor, and water met her feet.

What in the world? Still standing in the open doorway, she scanned the room for an explanation. The sound of running water came from upstairs. Was someone showering? Could her distraction have led her to the wrong house? That would be awkward. She glanced around once more to confirm the furniture looked familiar.

Then she spotted the issue across the room. Water dripping from the ceiling, running down a chandelier.

Something upstairs must be leaking. Heart thumping, Grace ran toward the staircase, but slipped onto her backside, then glided across the floor. "Oh no!"

"What's going on? Are you okay?" a man's voice called.

Grace rolled around to find Seth, the handyman, standing at the door. His chiseled face clean-shaven, a platter in his hands. Was it that scrumptious barbeque she'd smelled? She shook off the thoughts. Not important. There was a tsunami in Brooklyn's house to deal with.

She scrambled to get up, but slipped again. These stupid flip-flops were going in the trash. The soles were slick, making them like skates on ice. Seth set aside the plate and bent over her. He lifted her up to stand. "Are you hurt?"

Despite the calamity surrounding her, his sky-blue gaze halted her breathing for a split second, threatened to hold her mesmerized, and she fumbled for words. "I'm...I'm fine. We have to—"

A crash burst through her Seth-stare-trance as the kitchen light fixture hit the ground. A splat of sheetrock followed. Grace flung her arms around Seth's neck and shrieked. "Brooklyn's going to fire me. I don't know how, but I've destroyed the whole place, and I've only been in Santa Rosa a few hours." Tears choked her, blurring her vision. "I can't afford to get fired."

"You couldn't have caused this. I need to cut off the water, though." He stepped back and tipped her chin. "Can you stay in this spot? Like don't take one step?"

"Why? What if the ceiling crashes on me?"

"Good point." His gaze traveled upward. "I didn't want you to fall."

Again. Fall *again* is what he meant. "I'm used to falling. We have to do something to save the house."

Seth's forehead scrunched. "I don't—"

"I'll be fine. Let's hurry."

His brows lifted above those soulful eyes. "You hold onto me, and don't let go."

"Yes." The idea sounded disproportionately appealing considering the circumstances.

Arm in arm, they navigated the stairs to the second floor. The water appeared to be flowing from a guest bedroom, and she hadn't been in there. They splashed through the cold liquid and entered onto a squishy oriental rug. Then they came to a small bathroom beside the closet. The toilet gushed like a mini geyser.

"Oh, my goodness." She needed to cut the water off, ASAP. Releasing Seth, she lunged toward the back of the commode.

He held on, and they both flopped forward, feet slipping, her arms flailing.

They landed in a tangled mass on the floor, but she stretched and reached for the silver cutoff valve, turned it until the water slowed. "Why isn't it stopping?"

Shaking his head where he lay beside her on the tile floor, Seth laughed, that deep and hearty sound like the one she'd heard on the beach, as if this were what he did for fun every weekend. "You're hard-headed, too?"

Too? Something about the situation had her smiling despite the devastation. "I'm sorry. Are you okay?"

"Just wet." He scuffled to his feet and offered her a hand,

a smirk curling his full lips. "Do not let go this time."

"Got it." Don't let go of the hot guy, even to save the house. She took hold of his hand, squirmed up, and then slid her grip to his firm bicep. *Not thinking about the strength there. Much.*

They carefully made their way outside and found the meter.

"You may let go now." His voice held a smile.

"If you're sure." She complied, although she missed his warmth immediately.

"I have to go get a meter key next door to shut off the water. You can come if you want."

"I'll wait." She didn't want to come off as clingy, after all.

Not after she'd latched onto him all the way outside.

Why did she care if the man seemed to zap her dead heart to life? A nice, sweet handyman like Seth was probably married with children.

Maybe she'd ask Brooklyn when they talked. Grace's stomach sunk. And they'd have to talk soon. Oh, she dreaded the call she was about to make, trying to explain that *Clumsy Grace* hadn't been the one to explode the toilet in her boss's beach house.

Chapter 3

Seth couldn't stop his smile. Grace stood in the exact spot and position he had left her.

Good. She was safe. And cute. Soggy. Nibbling on her bottom lip, worry splattered over her expression. But cute.

He jogged to the water meter, knelt, and opened the metal cover. After extending the key, he turned the valve until it stopped. "We should be good. I'll call Brooklyn and explain what happened so she can get an insurance adjuster over."

"You'll call her? Will you tell her I didn't do it?" A divot formed between Grace's brows, pinching Seth's heart.

Huh. She must have quite the reputation for accidents. And he must be a sucker for a blue-eyed damsel. He'd always had a protective streak. "Of course, I'll explain. This mess is not your fault, Grace. Plumbing wears out. It happens more often than you think, especially near the salt water, and she's lucky we were here. Imagine if the place had been vacant."

"Oh." Her pert lips formed a circle. "I didn't think of it in that way." This news seemed to loosen the tension carved on her face.

The warmth in Seth's chest expanded. The pleasure he took in diminishing Grace's stress was way out of proportion. They'd known each other less than a day. "I'll make the call, then we'll get started with the cleanup."

"We?" Her thankful gaze worked like a valve in his heart releasing a larger torrent of pent-up emotions. Emotions like the ones he'd come to Santa Rosa to try to heal. Instead he'd simply escaped and hidden from the past, burying everything from his former life.

"Yes, *we*. And a crew of professionals I'm about to call."

Three hours later, Seth swiped his brow, took a deep slug of a Diet Coke he'd found in Brooklyn's refrigerator, and kept an eye on Grace. She'd been a trouper, following each instruction given. And not even falling again—only a few near misses. So far.

A strand of hair blew across her cheek as she carried a wet towel out to the deck. His thoughts made a path back to the feel of her in his arms. No one had been that physically close to him in a very long time. The contact had been nice.

More than nice.

His pulse raced, pounding in his ears. But, according to Brooklyn, Grace had travelled to Florida to recharge. He was pretty sure getting involved with another man—a damaged man—wasn't on her to-do list. He needed to get to work on the remodel project and keep his crazy feelings in check.

After Seth called the best restoration team in the area, the workers began to show up and start the process of cleaning up the water. They unplugged the appliances and electronics and set up huge fans. A few more guys arrived to carry out the wet rugs and cut away soaked drywall. They'd moved the furniture to the bedrooms not affected by the water, which meant a lot of pieces ended up in the master where Grace was planning to sleep. And that situation seemed like a disaster waiting to happen if she got up during the night. But there were no other choices at the moment. He'd just have to offer her a nightlight.

"We're done, Seth." Voice low and scratchy, Mac Strahan, the head of Mac's Plumbing, strode down the staircase beside the electrician. His work boots clomped under his long saggy jeans, and his fifty-year-old face showed more wear and wrinkles than it should. The man had given up smoking years before but still spent hours casting a line in the Florida sun. "We can come and check how the fans are drying the walls tomorrow. The insurance adjuster will be here first thing, and we took photographs of everything. We'll add Mrs. Barlow to our schedule. She said something about having her assistant be the point person for a remodel. She wanted to make a few cosmetic changes, too."

"She wants me to handle a remodel?" Grace's voice came from all the way out on the deck. She sure had good ears. Within seconds, she stood in front of them, eyes wide, her intense gaze bouncing between him and Mac. "I don't know much about construction."

A grin lifted Mac's bearded cheeks. "No need to worry, little lady. You got the hardware king right beside you. He's an expert."

Grace's gaze landed on Seth, a tentative smile twitching. "So, you're an expert? Are you a busy expert?"

Her teeth captured her bottom lip in the most adorable way while she waited for an answer.

As if he could say no. "I can help. I already volunteered, and Brooklyn's agreed."

Her gaze lifted to the ceiling. "Thank you, Lord."

Interesting. Maybe Grace was a believer. That would be another plus.

Not that he was counting.

~~~

What a crazy day. A weird and atrocious day, but somehow—she glanced at the house next door—bearable. Grace plopped into an iron recliner on the deck. The plumbing crew and the electrician had packed up and left, along with the other workers Seth had called to help. He'd walked the last man out to the street, and now the huge fans buzzing around the large home made it sound as if the place were full of giant swarming insects.

A hot soak in Brooklyn's elegant bathtub would be nice right about now, but with the water episode, the last thing she wanted to do was try the plumbing. What a mess. How was she going to manage a remodel on a place like this? Brooklyn was a great boss, but she had particular and exquisite style—the taste of the wealthy, not a middle-class girl from the suburbs.

Between that and finishing all the work Grace had brought with her, she wasn't sure she'd be able to handle everything that had been piled on her plate.

"Hey, I can microwave the food from hours ago, or we can eat out. Your call." The smooth, toasty voice tickled Grace's ears. Seth's voice.

Grace turned to find him in the open doorway, his lips pinched in a reserved smile, a slight dimple in his chin, both of which caused a spike in her pulse. "I thought you left."

"I needed to nail down the schedule for the week. The breakers are off for the power in the waterlogged portion of the house, by the way." He took a deep breath and then released it. "I haven't had dinner, but the steaks and shrimp have been sitting out for a while. I'm not dying to get food poisoning after all this." The moon hung low and large, and Seth's eyes shimmered a reflection of the light, sparking a fire that shot up Grace's neck and flooded her cheeks.

Was he asking her out to dinner? "I'm sorry about your food. The smell practically had me drooling before I walked into—" She waved her hand toward the house, catching the small metal table beside her and knocking it over. "Oops."

Quickly, Seth stepped over and righted the piece. He ran his hand over it checking for damage. "No harm done."

24

"Whew." She blew out a whistle. "Good." Even a lawn table belonging to Brooklyn would be expensive to replace.

"You're a piece of work." Chuckling, Seth moved closer. "Let's go out. What do you say?"

Tingles, like pricks of something akin to fuzzy caterpillars, walked across Grace's arms and shoulders. He *was* asking her to dinner. She certainly didn't want to be the other woman if he was married. She'd never do to another woman what her best friend had done to her. "What about your family? Aren't they expecting you at home?"

His smile faltered, and his face contorted for a ghost of a second before he recovered. His chin dipped. "There's not anyone waiting. I'm not married, if that's what you're asking."

His answer begged more questions, but she'd not press. "Well"—she shrugged—"one never knows these days."

"It's just dinner." The sparkle returned to his eyes. "You have to be starving."

She should be, but her stomach had gotten used to being neglected. Except for business lunches and those occasional chocolate-cherry-chunk-ice-cream binges, she often forgot to eat. Okay, maybe more than *occasional* ice cream binges, but at least she splurged on the high protein brand. "I'm game."

"There you go." He held out a hand to help her out of the recliner, as if he knew there might be an issue getting up. "Let's do it."

She accepted his assistance and pushed her feet to the decking. Bone weary, she stood. "Oh, I am no doubt in need of food."

"You're not going to pass out, are you?" Concern lifted his brows.

"That hasn't happened. My falls are completely unrelated to hunger. I've been tested for all sorts of disorders, and there's no explanation, other than maybe poor peripheral vision. My mom says I've always had my head in the clouds."

"I'm glad there's nothing worse to it." His brows lowered, and smile lines creased his temples. "What'll you have? Seafood, Italian, French, and don't say steak. I can cook a steak better than you can get at a restaurant, so we can grill another night."

Another night? Someone was getting a little ahead of himself. "I like everything. But, Seth—?"

"Yeah?"

"I haven't been out with a man alone since... my...divorce." How she loathed that word and the heart-crushing abandonment it ripped open. "It's been a while, but still—"

"Same here. With a woman, in my case." The anguish in the press of his lips pierced her reluctance.

"How long for you?" She swallowed past the thickness in her throat. "If you don't mind me asking."

"Three years."

"Oh." Maybe he understood. They might be able to offer each other some small encouragement. Like two passengers on a sinking ship. "Well, let's go eat."

"Let's." He offered his elbow, and she took it.

"Oh, wait." She glanced down at herself and let go of him. "I'm a mess. Is it safe to take a quick shower here?"

"It'll be fine. If not, just holler like you did earlier today. I'll hear you next door."

A laugh burst through her lips. "Will do. But my little shriek was nothing compared to the racket your saw made." She took a step away but stopped. "Are you staying next door while you remodel for the owners?"

One side of his mouth kicked up. "Something like that. I'll

meet you here in…what? Thirty minutes?"

"I'll see you then." Thirty minutes to shower and change. She better hurry. Her bags still lay unopened.

"And Grace."

"Yes." She turned to find him giving her a pointed—and slightly smoldering—stare.

"Be careful."

Easier said than done, in more ways than one.

Heart thumping and cheeks burning, she trashed her devious flip-flops with the rest of the bags of refuse. She'd buy another pair in town or go barefoot to the beach. But what clothes would she wear to dinner? She hadn't packed for a date. Not that this was a date. Or was it? Didn't matter. The outfits she'd brought for church were the nicest clothes in her bag, but even so, Brooklyn had said the congregation wore casual attire—jeans and a nice blouse. That would have to do. Her riding boots worked better than dress sandals for this season of the year, despite the warm weather. She laid out her favorite red shirt she'd found on sale at Nordstrom Rack, added her skinny jeans, and headed into the master bath.

Before undressing, she cautiously turned the faucet in the shower and held her breath. Perhaps she should make a quick patrol around the house to be sure there was no Niagara Falls action going on. After shutting the shower door, she tiptoed downstairs and surveyed the damaged kitchen. Oh, that hole in the ceiling was ugly. A long, silent moment passed with no geysers, volcanoes, or waterspouts. Not even a drip. She continued her tour of duty through all the rooms until she was sure the plumbing was secure. Finally, she returned to the bathroom, undressed, and let the hot water stream over her, washing away the muck and the stress of the day. Thank the Lord for clean, hot water. The little things she took for granted that were such blessings.

Her thoughts returned to the impending dinner. Now that Trevor had married, she felt like she could try dating. When she was honest with herself, she'd gotten over the lost romantic love. What haunted her were the betrayals and feelings of inadequacy, the *un-choosing* that had done an unravelling of her heart. The abandonment by those she'd trusted. The sting of going from being a couple to ordering take-out for one.

Dinner with a nice man could be a good thing. A first step toward building a new life. Not that anything serious would come of tonight other than food and conversation, but now was as good a time as any, and Santa Rosa as good a place as any, to start rebuilding her confidence.

~~~

Seth stared at himself in the mirror and buttoned his collared shirt. What had he been thinking? Cooking food for a neighbor was one thing. Taking an attractive, single woman to a popular restaurant was a whole other set of nuts and bolts. He mostly ate his meals at home for a reason. In town, families would be out and about, and he never knew when grief would sink its jagged talons into his heart and crush his mood. Or worse.

Most days he functioned well enough, a familiar numbness allowing him to take care of business, shop, and walk the beach to relax. Other days, the slightest event could trigger flashbacks to those devastating times—paramedics, shock, paperwork, tears, arguments, decisions, and finally, the bureaucracy of death..

Chapter 4

Seth's knock at the door seemed to propel a flock of seagulls into flight in Grace's stomach. She was really doing this. *Okay, feet, go answer the door without falling.*

At the French door, he waited, shifting his weight from one foot to another. Maybe he was as nervous as she was.

Here goes. Grace turned the knob and swung open the door. "Hi."

His pressed blue button-down brought out the color of his eyes. "Ready?" A smile tugged at the corners of his lips, the glow from the landscape light accentuating the symmetric angles of his cheekbones and defined chin with that notched dimple.

She managed a nod. *Ready as I'll ever be.*

A shiny red Nissan Titan hummed in the drive. Seth escorted her out and opened the passenger door. The inside of the truck gleamed almost as brightly as the outside. The man obviously loved his vehicle.

On the drive over, a subdued version of Seth gave her the rundown on the area including where to purchase food and other necessities. Twinkling lights and red bows adorned the adorable town with its tiny post office and quaint shops along brick-lined avenues. After the tour of that central area, they cruised down a dark highway until they reached the bay. Seth shared stories about learning to fish there with his grandparents. The casual conversation calmed a smidgen of the nerves swirling in her stomach. She hadn't dated anyone

29

besides Trevor since her sophomore year of college, so she hadn't been alone with another guy for a long time. And she'd never been a pro at the whole playing-the-game thing. If this was a date. And she still wasn't sure it was.

After parking, Seth quickly circled the truck to open her door. A cool breeze caught her hair and sent a shiver down her arms. Either that or the chills were thanks to her cute escort.

"Rain may be coming soon." Seth motioned for her to go ahead of him across the white rocks covering the lot and up the boardwalk to the restaurant entrance. He opened the door and waited until she'd gone through, then he caught the attention of the hostess. "Seth, party of two."

That sounded really nice...better than, *Grace, party of one.*

A hostess seated them, took a drink order, and offered menus.

"Do you like shrimp, oysters, and fish? They have a great platter we could share. Then we'll have room for pie." His brows raised and lowered. "They have an awesome key lime or peanut butter. I mean top of the heap."

"You're speaking my native language. Desserts-first 101." Trevor never would've split a meal. Taking a french fry from his plate was a punishable offense. He guarded his plate as if it were his death-row last meal.

Grace held in a chuckle. Sharing a spicy seafood platter in a cozy, upscale restaurant with an attractive guy was not how she'd expected to spend her first evening in Santa Rosa. Of course, she hadn't expected an exploding toilet either.

The view from the large window near their table overlooked a bay. Stars twinkled in the dark purple skies, and the moon reflected on the tranquil waters. A candle flickered on their table, and glowing white Christmas lights adorned the walls, creating cheer.

The food ordered and delivered, they both dug in, first adding fried oysters to their plates.

"You love these, too?" Seth asked, brows raised. "A lot of people don't."

"If they're cooked nice and crispy like my dad's."

"Same here."

Grace couldn't stop a smile. They seemed to have a lot in common.

A young man with a brown goatee crooned a mellow song to the strum of his guitar, and she forked her first bite. Yum. The batter had been perfectly fried.

"How long did you plan to stay in Santa Rosa before you were put in charge of the unexpected remodel?" The lights reflected in Seth's eyes, his gaze kind and unassuming.

"I have to be in Atlanta in early January when the legislature convenes. Things get really crazy for several months."

"You aren't going home for Christmas?" His face dipped while he squeezed a third slice of lemon into his sweet tea and stirred.

"I don't know." A shard of insecurity slashed into Grace's spirits. "My family means well with their advice and all, but..."

"You don't have to explain. I've been there." Setting aside his drink, Seth met her gaze, smirked, and made air quotes. "Like, 'time heals all wounds,' or 'at least you weren't married thirty years. You're young. You can start over.'" His Adam's apple bobbed, his fingers clenched. "As if any of that helps."

"Exactly." He *did* get it. "My mom actually said, 'I knew he would do something like this one day. I just had that feeling.' And then my sister added, 'I don't know what you ever saw in him in the first place. You're better off without him.'" She huffed. "I mean, they could've spoken up before I married him

31

if they'd noticed red flags, you know?"

His blue eyes widened as he took in the statements which had only served to more thoroughly shatter her broken heart. "That was a few years late and a few-thousand divorce-lawyer dollars short." He took a swig of his tea and swallowed, his expression contemplative. "Here's one. A coworker asked me if we'd tried counseling because 'he and his wife had issues but had worked hard to make it.' I felt like saying, 'No, I'd just rather pay exorbitant amounts to attorneys to have my heart ripped out of my chest.'" His broad shoulders lifted as if his statement were a nonchalant one. "But I didn't say it." He chuckled, though the sound was anything but amused. "It's possible I might've struggled with anger issues."

Hadn't she wanted to shout at Trevor and Alexa? Scream about how badly they'd hurt her? Instead, she'd squashed down that heap of outrage, tucked it somewhere in a hollow place they'd dredged out. "I wanted to be angry, but I kept trying to understand. I kept wondering—asking myself over and over—if something stupid I'd done or said sent my husband into the arms of my best friend."

His expression softened. "I'm sorry." Seth reached across the table, and his fingers covered hers. Strong, calloused fingers that both calmed and electrified her. "That's just wrong, and in no way was it your fault. You *should* have some righteous anger over a betrayal like that." He gave her hand a squeeze. "I don't mean for you to stay angry, but feel the emotion, so you can move forward. Yes, Christians forgive, but we are still allowed emotions." His brows rose above those kind blue eyes. "I'm sorry to make an assumption. That you are a believer."

Tears pricked Grace's eyes. So, Seth was a man of faith. Probably a question she should've asked before this adventure, but the offer had taken her off guard.

"I am a believer," she said. "And thank you for that good advice." A wave of peace settled over her like a favorite quilt. She'd chosen to go out to dinner with someone she'd just met, but at least they had their faith in common. Maybe she'd call Brooklyn and find out more about Seth...Seth... Wait, what was his last name? She hadn't asked, and if he'd told her, she'd forgotten. How awkward. She really was out of practice. If she was going to date, perhaps she should make a checklist. Faith and last name would be the first two questions. Mandatory questions.

~~~

Grace is a Christian.

That news washed over Seth and buoyed his spirits like a lighthouse materializing on a murky night at sea. If he'd married a woman who'd shared his faith the first time, maybe they could've survived what happened. He'd thought Selina would come to believe eventually. She'd been willing to attend worship services with him, go to a small group, but she'd never given her life to the Lord. Overcoming the shock and sting of death without the belief in a resurrection had broken her. Their baby boy dying had broken him, too, but he'd known God was there in the midst of the anguish. This life wasn't all there was. He still believed, even if he didn't understand.

"Any other funny advice you want to share?" Grace's voice floated through Seth's consciousness.

He'd almost let himself slip into that stale, dark place.

The lift of Grace's pert lips brought out those smile lines he'd noticed, and her deep blue eyes sparkled even brighter in the shimmering Christmas lights. An uplifting sight if ever there was one.

"Okay, digging deep." He grappled through his memory to divorce advice, weeding out the awkward things that had been said after they'd lost Noah. "A friend told me, 'I hope I don't get divorced, too.' As if it were contagious."

A small chuckle drifted across the table, widening Grace's smile. "People mean well, though. I never know what to say to hurting people either. Other than 'I'm sorry you're going through this,' you know, whatever it is."

"Perfect thing to say."

Her eyes met his, and she giggled. "I guess it's better than, 'When are you going to start dating? Can I set you up? I know a nice guy who's getting divorced.'"

Seth let his head fall forward, and he laughed hard. "Oh, yeah. I get that a lot. Well, except it's a nice girl."

"At least we can laugh about that junk now."

"I haven't laughed this much in—" How long had it been? "It seems like another life." Laughter had only existed in the life of blissful ignorance he'd led before he'd found Noah that morning in the crib. Ignorance that someone so perfect could be snatched away without warning. Ignorance that the death of one so tiny could rip apart two lives and what he'd thought was a strong marriage. A lump clogged his throat. Seth blasted the memory away. He had to stop torturing himself. It wasn't his fault. The doctor had explained the autopsy conclusions— more than once—to Selina and to him.

His gaze drifted to Grace. If nothing else, tonight had shown him that somewhere under his grief, his heart still beat. "Thank you for coming, Grace. I've enjoyed this."

"Me, too." The tenderness in her gaze tore away more of the boarded-up places inside his soul. "And you were right about the desserts. Definitely works of culinary art." She nodded toward the empty plates.

The waitress delivered the bill, Seth cleared the tab, and then he offered Grace his hand. "Would you like to walk out on the pier before we head back? It's a nice night."

"Why not? As long as you keep me from falling overboard, my work can wait a few more hours."

"I got you covered. And work?" He pulled her forward and chuckled. "What's that? Come on. After the mess we cleaned up earlier, you need to enjoy yourself."

She followed. "Easy for you to say. What exactly is your job, Mr., um, Mr.—"

"Oh, wow." He pivoted her way and pinned Grace with a playful stare. "You don't know my last name, do you?"

Her cheeks pinked as her smile faltered. "Did you tell me? Mine's Grace Logan, by the way. It seems our introductions were not the norm. I'm usually pretty good with names. Names are important in the lobbying business."

"Our meetings have definitely been straight-up weird, so maybe I didn't tell you." He gave a half-bow. "Seth Gibbs, at your service. And I'm a tool guy." Waggling his brows, he added. "Maybe in more ways than one. Like, I'm a tool, get it? Do people say that anymore?"

"Only tools." Those cute lips twisted to hold back a grin, then she toppled forward. "Whoa!"

Seth caught her around the waist and pulled her close before she did any damage. "You are much too hazardous for your own good."

"Thanks. My heel caught on that nail. I can find something to stumble over anywhere." Blue eyes gazed up at him. She was so close, he could study the long lashes framing them as they lowered. "Maybe that's why he chose someone else over me."

Seth's heart squeezed. How some jerk left her feeling like that, he couldn't imagine. And he couldn't help tipping her chin to pull her gaze toward his. "If there's one thing I know after only one day, you are not to blame." His fingers traced her soft jawline, traveled to cup her cheeks, while his eyes locked onto those lips. He inhaled the soft hint of a peppermint after-dinner mint on her shallow breath. His pulse surged while his breathing halted. He shouldn't, but he couldn't stop bending toward her, closing his eyes, and caressing her lips with his own.

He tasted softness and tenderness, passion and beauty, the scents of lilac and sea air filling his senses. Lost for a long moment, he explored her lips, until finally, he lifted his head, still cradling her face.

Grace's lashes fluttered open, and her eyes locked with his.

"I probably shouldn't have done that." Seth's voice came out husky. As a matter of fact, he knew he shouldn't have.

Chapter 5

Oh, man, he'd messed up.

Seth's breathing stalled, the band of muscles in his torso locking into a tight vise. Reality submerged him further into a current of churning regret. He shouldn't have started a romantic relationship when he didn't have the emotional fortitude to follow through. Especially without knowing more about Grace's hopes and dreams for the future.

"I'm sorry," Grace whispered and touched her pink lips.

"Why in the world are you sorry?" He let the pad of his thumb run down her cheek. "I'm the one who seems to have lost my senses." Unraveling what he'd started would be tricky. "You probably think I'm some player now. The truth is, you're the first woman I've kissed since Selina." Whoops. Didn't mean to mention her either. Too late. He shrugged one shoulder. "My ex."

"First one?" Her blue gaze searched his face and plunged deep into his heart. Had he truly only known this woman one day? He managed a nod.

"Mine, too." She blew out an embarrassed huff. "I mean, since Trevor."

Seth pulled her into a warm embrace, and whispered next to her ear, "Well, it was the perfect first kiss, if you ask me." The feel of her in his arms cracked something inside, something buried deep and cold. He didn't want to let her go, but he had no choice. Slowly releasing her, he cleared his throat. "Maybe a bit too soon, since we've only just met."

Her lashes fluttered again. "Right."

His abs tightened as if waiting for a harsh blow. If she cried, it would kill him.

One side of her mouth quirked up. "Hmm, I guess that was a pretty good one."

Grace was a class act. "Pretty good?" He gave her a playful nudge but fought the urge to replay the whole exquisite experience in living color right this very second. But continuing the flirtations wouldn't be fair to either of them. "I need to tell you—"

"Oh, look!" Grace stepped away from his hold and made quick steps down the boardwalk toward the parking lot. "Carolers in costume."

Voices flowed from the group of about twenty singers, some dressed in white choir robes. They performed *Away in a Manger.* As Seth followed Grace toward the gathering, his throat thickened, making it hard to swallow. Where had they come from? This restaurant's location wasn't near the heart of town.

In the center of the singers, three shepherds and three wise men surrounded a young couple dressed as Mary and Joseph. The stranglehold on Seth's throat tightened.

They held an infant, maybe four months old. The child let out a shrill cry, and his mother gently lifted him to her shoulder.

The baby's wail reverberated in Seth's ears, split open that hollowed-out place in his soul, spilling out the grief and ache that slashed through him every time he saw an infant near Noah's age.

Every time the day of his son's birth circled around. Every time the anniversary of the day they'd lost him arrived shrouded in darkness and sorrow.

The ache in his arms, the cries that haunted him in his dreams, threatened to drown him in a sea of guilt.

Pain coiled in his chest, and his pulse raced. He had to get out of here.

"Grace, I have to go. Now."

~~~

What happened? Grace turned from the singers to glimpse Seth practically jogging to his truck.

Confusion and disappointment collided in her heart. Was he ill? Was it the kiss? Had she done or said some other klutzy thing for the millionth time in her life?

She made a beeline to the passenger door but paused before pulling the handle. Did he want to give her a ride?

Though Seth stood at the driver's side, he seemed to catch himself. He rounded the truck, clicked the key fob, and opened her door, then waited for her to get in.

Grace braved a glance at his stony face as she stepped up and took a seat. Oh, for a spine of steel to manage the urges warring inside—one, to curl up in tears. Another, to run away. And the last, to put a comforting arm around Seth.

The door closed, and he entered on his side, cranked the vehicle, and started down the dark road, leaving the Christmas scene behind.

Other than the hum of the engine and the pounding of Grace's pulse, complete and utter silence filled the cab. Should she ask what was wrong, or wait for him to speak?

Questions barraged her as the minutes and miles passed. Still nothing.

"Seth? Are you all right?" Although she hoped he wasn't ill, pathetically, that answer would make her feel better about herself. How selfish was that?

Hunched toward the steering wheel, he gave a single nod

and cleared his throat. "I need to get home." His Adam's apple bobbed with a hard swallow. "Sorry."

"Don't be sorry. You can't help how you feel." Grace stared across the dimly lit cab, waiting for something more. Anything. But again, silence.

Could their food have made him sick? Lines burrowed into Seth's forehead, and there was tightness of his angled jaw.

She should be quiet and leave him be. For the rest of her visit to Santa Rosa.

But the house and all that mess...

Inwardly, Grace groaned. If Seth was sick, she'd handle whatever she had to about the water issue. She'd been learning to take care of life without the help of a man for a while. This latest disaster would be no different.

Maybe he wasn't ill at all. Maybe he just really regretted kissing her.

Finally, they reached her driveway, and Seth punched in the code for the gate. He must've taken care of many household issues for Brooklyn if he knew the code. The truck came to a stop, and she popped open the door.

"Grace, wait." Seth faced her, at last, and sighed, clearly uncomfortable. "I owe you an explanation."

"I hope you feel better." The last thing she wanted was someone's pity. She stepped out of the truck. "You don't owe me anything."

Chapter 6

Bleary-eyed, Seth stared in the mirror the next morning. Wrestling with his demons all night had stolen his sleep but not accomplished much else. That hearty infant cry from the evening before had haunted him. He longed with every fiber of his being to hear a lusty wail from his little Noah again. If he could go back and be that anxious new father, trying to soothe those cries with gentle crooning, digging deep to pull up the lyrics of long-forgotten nursery rhymes and lullabies.

He pressed his lids shut only to feel a sense of free-falling from a towering cliff. Shortness of breath, vertigo, and the racing pulse. He jerked his eyes back open. The symptoms he suffered in these moments had been diagnosed as "mild" post-traumatic stress.

How had one dark night stolen so much?

Seth pulled a clean shirt over his head and clomped, barefoot, downstairs to press the button on the coffee maker. Likely the first brew of many today. The journal his sister-in-law had given him lay open on the counter, his scribbling attempts at working through his rocky jumble of emotions. After grabbing his cup of coffee, he tucked the journal under his arm and headed to the deck.

Outside, a chill clung to the misty, early morning air, though the first rays of sunrise streamed across the rolling Gulf waves. The American flag attached to the railing of Brooklyn's crow's nest flapped in the cool breeze. What must Grace think of him? He took a deep swig of coffee and sat at the outdoor table, the metal chair nippy even through his jeans. Setting his cup aside, he opened the journal to where a pen marked the place he'd left off.

Writing was supposed to be cathartic, so he'd tried, but he often felt as though he was only succeeding in waging war with his sanity. Might as well take another stab at it because if last night were any indication, something needed to give.

He lifted the pen and wrote.

Some days, it seems my heart stopped beating when Noah's did. Perhaps Selina's had, as well, and that's why she could never get past the loss. Or past the guilt and blame and anger. Could never love or forgive me.

Though my arms ache to hold him and my mind pounds with unanswered questions, I need to find a new normal. I want to find a way to remember the gift from God that Noah was. I don't want the focus from myself, my family, or my friends to be on "Seth's baby who died." I want Noah to be remembered as that cooing little boy who smiled and drooled and lived, if only for a few short months. Despite the sea of death's grief, I want to remember the life.

How do I do that, though? How do I move forward and start a new life without fear, God? How were You able to give up Your son, Lord?

I know You are constant and good. I need Your help to find my way. To share my story. But how? How do I share my story with others...with Grace? Is it fair to ask Grace or any woman to bear the heavy baggage of my pain?

Slamming truck doors interrupted his deliberations. Seth closed the journal, stood, and ventured down the steps toward Brooklyn's house. Already, the electrician stood knocking, waiting for Grace to answer. The plumber pulled up behind him.

Good grief, they were out early. He needed to get over there, but not without shoes. Too many broken shells had sliced into his heels the first year he'd moved here.

Brooklyn's side door swung open, and Seth's breath caught. Wispy strands of Grace's honey-brown hair hung around her face while the rest poked out of a clip that allowed a nice view of her slender neck. Listening to the workman talk, she pressed her index finger against her lips.

Those lips.

Last night's kiss slammed into his mind.

Electricity inundated his senses, sent tingles down his empty arms. Waking up to a sweet woman like Grace could be worth taking a risk and sharing his story.

Though he'd determined to live unmarried and alone, meeting her yesterday had opened up an intense longing for companionship...and so much more. A partner for life, an intimate relationship, a best friend, a helpmate. He longed for the commitments and promises and blessings that marriage offered. Could that be possible someday? Maybe with the right woman. A woman who wasn't hoping to start a family.

As if drawn by some magnetic force, Grace's eyes found him. She offered a quick wave and looked away.

He had to figure out how to make things right. He'd really blown it last night.

~ ~ ~

She wouldn't look in Seth's direction again.

Grace ran her fingers across her makeup-free, puffy morning face. How awful that he'd seen her like this. Last night had been humiliating enough. So much for building up her confidence. If this first date after her divorce was any indication of how starting over was going to go, she'd rather stay single.

After grabbing the pad and pen from her computer bag, she focused on the instructions the electrician and plumber

43

spouted as they walked around the house. Sleeping had proved almost impossible after the romantic dinner and impromptu out-of-this-world kiss, then the abrupt and bizarre ride home. All that added to the early hour left her brain foggy and in need of coffee.

Except, apparently the coffee maker had been a casualty of falling sheetrock. And now, the power needed to be cut off in the entire kitchen as well as much of the rest of the house, including the room where the modem was connected. How would she work without the internet? Or caffeine?

The first order of business would be to locate a coffee shop. If Brooklyn said it was okay to leave the workers alone in the house, Grace might take her computer and hang out there. Away from Mr. Wonderful-Incredible-Kisser-But-Possibly-Crazy-Hot-Guy.

"You got all that, little lady? Or do we need to wait for Mr. Gibbs's approval?" Mac-the-plumber's scratchy voice grated on her nerves.

Little lady? Since graduating from the University of Georgia and joining Brooklyn's staff, she'd learned how to assert herself among high-powered businessmen and politicians without being unpleasant. The same principles should apply with construction crews, right?

"I don't need his approval." Although his advice would've been helpful, he surely wouldn't show his face again. She held up the pad. "I have my notes, and as soon as I can get on the internet with access to a fax and a printer, I'll produce a simple contract for both parties to sign." Outside the window, more workers parked in the drive and along the street. A whole parade of men would have to move their vehicles for her to back out.

"Well, aren't you efficient?" Mac tipped his hat. "I need a

good administrative assistant like you in my office."

Maybe he wasn't so bad after all. Just a little rough around the edges. "Thanks. Is there a business center within walking distance?" A mild headache already throbbed in her temples. "And a coffee shop?"

Mac pointed toward the opening door. "You may not need his approval, but you might want his coffee and internet."

There stood Seth, his strong shoulders and profile outlined by the hazy light hovering on the horizon. As he stepped closer, the touch of scruff on his face gave him a far-too-appealing, rugged-morning vibe that set off multiple warning alarms in her mind. Danger ahead.

"Hi." A tentative smile lifted his lips, and he offered a silver go-cup. "Can you step outside a moment?"

If it weren't for the delightful coffee aroma, her good sense might have listened to those alarms. But they didn't. Okay, maybe his striking-but-apologetic blue eyes convinced her to follow him, too. Grace took the coffee and scooted past the men who seemed to be setting up camp in the kitchen.

On the stoop, she stopped, took a sip of the hot brew, and stared out at the frothy ocean. The wind kicked up, humidity practically dangling in the air. Clouds rolled in, dark and ready for the bottom to fall out any minute.

"I'm Seth Gibbs. Can we make a new start?" Seth gave her a sad-puppy face if there ever was one and held out his hand for her to shake. "As friends and temporary neighbors? Oh, and toilet-repair-and-remodeling project partners."

Her faith wouldn't allow her to hold a grudge, but Seth had been the one to suggest that Christians should feel their emotions. And her emotions were wounded with a touch of bewildered. A tad miffed, too. "I'm confused." And fearful of how her body would respond, so she ignored his hand.

45

"Of course you are. I flaked out." His hand dropped, and he shoved both into his jeans' pockets, his gaze falling to the ground. "The way I acted had nothing to do with you. Long story I don't want to go into right this second, but my behavior was brought on by the carolers." His eyes mashed shut, so did his lips.

Pain pressed there in his expression. She recognized that much. Did he know one of the singers? All sorts of crazy scenarios entered her mind. His ex-wife was in the group. A horrific caroling experience as a child left him scarred. Supersonic hearing made him vulnerable to high-pitched noises. He had an unreasonable fear of people in costumes.

"What do you say?" His eyes opened, and his penetrating stare roamed her face, drawing her in and overrunning her efforts to remain aloof.

She held out her hand. "I'm Grace Logan. Nice to meet you. Can I use your internet and a printer?" Hopeful, she lifted her brows. "Maybe drink a bunch of your coffee and pick your brain about remodeling? I hear tell you're a tool guy."

His calloused fingers took her hand and gave a firm shake. Heat radiated from his fingers and his broad smile. "Or maybe just a tool. But yes to all of the above."

And yes, her hand was on fire from his touch, but she would ignore her crazy feelings for her new friend and temporary neighbor. At least until she could get out of the driveway.

Chapter 7

Come on, brain, clear the fog. Grace Logan, you're an intelligent woman.
Stop with all the mushiness.

She had to let go of Seth's hand and regain use of her mouth. Her fingers throbbed, but that didn't compare to the bass drum pounding in her ribcage. There had been something she needed to find before she trekked next door with the man. "I needed coffee and...and..."

Blinking, Seth shook his head and released her. "Creamer? Sugar? Internet?"

"Internet." That was it. Glad his mind still worked, she took one step forward but then stopped. "It would help if I brought my computer." A hair straightener and makeup would've been nice too, but no time for primping.

Seth laughed, that hearty sound she'd loved. "Good thinking. I'll—" He turned on the stoop, but one foot caught on the other, and he stumbled, then dropped to one knee with a thud against the wooden decking. "Ouch."

"Are you okay?" She leaned beside him.

His cheeks reddened, as he stood and then recovered with a sheepish smile. "Just injured pride. I'll wait here and recuperate while you get your laptop."

"Pride?" She couldn't stop a chuckle after she felt assured he was fine. "Remember you're with Clumsy-Grace. No worries about pride."

"Hey." His voice was barely above a whisper. "I'll not have you calling yourself by that name. If you have to add an

47

adjective, go with Beautiful Grace or Intelligent Grace."

Her cheeks blazed, likely turning as red as a bowl of her favorite Pace Picante Sauce. "I'll pass on the modifiers. Be right back." She measured her steps to be sure she wouldn't have a similar mishap, especially with the comings and goings of worker-men plus the equipment inside the house. Once she gathered her laptop, her purse, and phone, while balancing the precious cup of java, Grace filled her lungs with a greatly needed breath of oxygen, held it, then slowly released the air. A grown woman could use the internet and drink coffee at a neighbor's for a little while, couldn't she?

A neighbor whose dreamy-steamy kiss had kept her tossing and turning all night.

Maybe a quick call to Brooklyn was in order. Just to be sure. A grown woman still needed to be careful.

She punched in her boss's number.

"Good morning, Grace. Were you able to rest after the drama last night?"

"Drama?" Her pulse skipped. What drama did Brooklyn know about? Had Seth told her about the kiss-and-run debacle?

"The water breaking through the ceiling drama?"

Duh. "Right. I'm fine." Of course, he wouldn't have told Brooklyn the awkward rest of the story. "The coffee pot was practically flattened, and the internet is out, so do you think it's safe for me to hang out next door? To use the internet?" And drink as much coffee as humanly possible in the short span of time she planned to spend there.

"At Seth's?" A peculiar snicker laced Brooklyn's voice. "He's as safe as a teddy bear, and just as sweet. Poor baby. He's had a tough go of it, and his family worries about him. I'd hoped you two would meet when I sent you down there."

Her boss was giggling? "Right. Okay." A teddy bear was not how she wanted to imagine Seth. Not that she should be imagining him at all.

"It would be incredible if you would spend time with him. You're strong and kind and secure in your faith, Grace. I know you can help Seth."

Something fishy was going on. "You know his family? I thought he was a handyman doing construction next door."

"He's handy all right. Comes from a long line of handy Gibbs Hardware men. They're part of the Hardware Association."

A lump formed in Grace's throat. "The Gibbs Hardware Stores? Like the North American chain based in Atlanta?"

"What other would there be?" Brooklyn's voice returned to the usual brisk business tone.

He did say he was a tool guy. But he didn't make it clear how many tools he was talking about. And she'd thought he was... "I better get to work."

"Keep me up to date." Brooklyn cleared her throat. "On everything and everyone."

The implication hung between them. Her boss seemed to be trying to take up matchmaking. Not the kind of issue Brooklyn normally took the time to lobby. The woman centered her life around her business and supporting causes she was passionate about in an attempt to stay sane after grief and loss. If Brooklyn felt sorry for Seth, his story must be tragic.

~~~

Shoot. That hurt. Seth blew out a long breath. How long had it been since he'd taken a spill? High school football, maybe? And that was deliberate falling. His mind must really be off-kilter today. Or since he'd met Grace. He shifted his

49

weight to his non-injured side. The pain where his foot twisted far outweighed the throbbing where his knee hit the decking. But neither compared to the ache in the vicinity of his heart when he'd seen the bewildered look on Grace's face both last night and again this morning.

At least she'd allowed them to clear the air so they could start over and move forward. As friends. They'd only just met anyway. And it wouldn't be fair to waste her time on a romantic relationship that had no future. She was younger than he was. Even if she said she didn't care about having children, she might change her mind in a few years.

He couldn't chance that nightmare again. His heart couldn't bear the loss of another child.

Thunder rumbled overhead, drawing his gaze skyward. If she didn't hurry, they'd be wet.

"I'm back." Grace's sweet, perky voice pierced his weather assessments. A smile lifted her lips, a place his eyes longed to linger, but with a good shove of mental effort he was able to pry his gaze away, only to be sucked into staring at her luminous blue eyes.

Blinking, Grace toed the wood below her feet while he stood there speechless. "I'm ready to drink more coffee, bum your Wi-Fi to download some docs, and use your printer, too, if you have one."

Stop gawking. "I'm your guy." Seriously? "Your guy for Wi-Fi, a printer, and coffee, I mean. I have plenty more where that came from." Good grief. Just hit mute.

A chuckle slipped through those adorable lips. "That'll do. I should be able to get access to more when I can back out of the driveway. I'll replace Brooklyn's coffee maker when I find the store."

"I have an extra brewer next door you can have."

50

"You bring your own to every job?" Her arched brows lifted, and her mouth twitched after speaking.

If they'd been playing cards, she'd be easy to read. His brothers had always loved a rowdy game of Rook, and they loved to try to bluff. Obviously, Grace knew he wasn't a construction worker, but he could still have a few more minutes messing with her. "Not all of them." Of course, maybe he'd messed with her enough already.

"Just the long-term, luxury beach house situations?" Her voice held a tease, so maybe she was okay playing the game a bit longer.

He gave a single nod. "Something like that. Let's go get you set up." Pointing as he took a step, he led her forward. The pain in the side of his foot almost earned a wince, but he held it in. No sense worrying her. If it still bothered him later, he'd ice it.

Silence crept between them and slid down Seth's shoulders. Ignoring the tension from the previous evening proved more difficult than he'd imagined. Especially if Grace would be hanging around his house for the day. He could ignore his online work and finish his projects in the garage, leaving her inside.

Lightning sliced the air, and thunder cracked, loudly this time. Grace squealed as fat raindrops poured from the clouds, slapping their faces and arms.

"Run!" Seth placed a hand on the small of her back and led her at a jog across the brick sidewalk, despite the ache still throbbing in his foot. Please don't let Grace bite the dust, Lord.

They reached his deck, and he opened the door, offering her first entry. "Careful on the tile." One of his next projects would be to lay hardwood instead of the slippery ceramic floors. Whoever had done the interior design for the beach

51

house must not have ever walked around with wet feet on this stuff.

Thankfully, Grace didn't seem to have any trouble. So far. He shut the door and followed her footsteps. Maybe too closely. He slid on the water dripping from her, and his foot darted out from under him, leaving him on the floor, contorted worse than if he'd been in a game of Twister gone wrong. Pain ripped through his foot when he fumbled to stand. "Ow—oh—" Some choice words fumbled toward his lips that didn't need to come out of a Christian man's mouth. "Oh, fiddlesticks!"

He'd never broken a bone, but there was no ignoring the throbbing agony on the right side of his foot. He needed to get himself to a doctor.

Chapter 8

That had to hurt.

Grace's heart flipped in her chest as she knelt beside Seth. With a groan, he'd removed his shoe. A line of purple already ran along the outer edge of his foot, and it had begun to swell. "Where are your keys? We need to get you to an emergency room for x-rays."

"There's a rack." The words came clipped from between clenched teeth. "On the way to the garage. We'll pass it."

"When you're ready, lean on me, and I'll help you get there." Cautious, she placed a hand on his shoulder.

"You don't have to. I can..." He glanced around as if seeking other options.

Maybe he didn't want her to take him. "Is your family down here?"

He shook his head. "They're in San Diego for a grand opening."

"Then I'm taking you, unless you want me to call an ambulance." She still held her phone but had set aside her computer bag and her purse when he'd fallen. She slung her purse back over her shoulder.

"No ambulance." His eyes squeezed closed.

"While you get mentally prepared to move, I'll find the keys and an icepack. Maybe a towel or pillow to prop it up." She stood, glancing around the house. "Your wallet with the insurance info?"

"Wallet by my bed. It's down the hall off the kitchen, first door you come to. Pillow there. Icepack in freezer." Each sentence was clipped out with obvious pain.

"I'll get everything." She stopped in the kitchen, grabbed an icepack, then followed a short hall to the master bedroom. If circumstances and weather had been different, she would've been wowed by the wall of windows that allowed a spectacular view of the beach. The wallet lay right where he'd described, but beneath it lay a turned-down picture frame. She picked up the wallet, but curiosity held her fingers over the picture.

What was she thinking? Whatever the frame held was none of her business, and this was an emergency.

She grabbed a pillow from the bed and jogged through the kitchen to a door with a rack neatly holding a multitude of labeled keys. The Nissan Titan keys had a gold ring with a metal tag that had *Gibbs Hardware* inscribed across it.

She opened the door to the garage and gawked. Every square inch of wall held racks and shelves lined with tools, saws, equipment, and wood. Even some scrap metal.

Go. She didn't have time for this. She placed the pillow and icepack on the far side of the back seat. Seth could lie there with his foot propped up. His wallet and her phone she threw on the passenger seat, and then she turned toward the house.

"I'm almost there." Seth had literally crawled to meet her. He rose on his knees at the doorframe. "I need help standing to get in the truck though."

"I've got you." She snaked a hold around his waist. "Put your arm over my shoulder."

His hand rested on her back, but he hesitated. "Are you sure you don't need to go get someone next door? I don't want to hurt you."

The tenderness in his voice, considering his current state of pain, melted her heart. Most people would be irritable and snippy in this situation. Well, Trevor would've been, anyway. "I'm stronger than I look. And despite many tumbles, I've never broken, dislocated, torn, or sprained anything." She tried to sound reassuring. "My mother swears I'm made of rubber and springs. Like Tigger."

"Okay, Tigger, if you're sure." A sort-of smile lifted his lips, and he leaned his weight into her, using his good leg to stand. They shuffled down the stoop, and he stopped. "If I hold your arm, I think I can hop on one foot to the truck."

"Won't that—?"

His hand slid to her bicep, and he hopped, then sucked in a breath. "Hopping hurts. It jolts. Was that what you were going to say?"

"Maybe. I set up a pillow and ice in the back seat. We're close."

"I'll make it." With a couple more steps leaning against her, his jaw tight, he reached the truck door. Allowing room for it to open proved tricky, but finally, he sat and swung his legs onto the seat.

"I'll go to the other side, prop your foot, and place the ice." She shut him in and jogged around.

He'd removed his other shoe, and his feet already rested on the pillow. Thankfully the icepack had a cover on it, so they didn't need a towel. She stared at the bruising on the outside of his foot.

"I know, I know. I should've gotten a pedicure, right." Seth wiggled his good foot, obviously trying to relieve the tension. "If only I'd known a pretty girl would be checking out my feet."

"I'm not..." Oh, goodness, he was funny and cute even when he was injured. She met his gaze. "I don't know how to put on the ice without hurting you."

"Maybe, lift my leg and put the pack under my foot. It's pliable. We sell them at our stores."

Her lips twitched at his mention of their family business. "Your stores?"

"Gibbs Hardware. Maybe you've heard of them?" He shrugged. "And I'm pretty sure Brooklyn or Mac told you. Don't play poker, lady. You have a tell."

"What tell?" Gingerly, she lifted his calf and slid the icepack beneath.

"Your lips twitch when you lie."

"Lie? I haven't lied. If anyone did, it would be you." She set his foot down.

A groan slipped from Seth, and he grimaced.

"Oh, sorry." Her heart skittered, and her every muscle froze. "I didn't mean to."

Rolling his eyes, he shook his head. "Call a dying man a liar? That's brutal."

Was he joking to make her feel better when she'd actually hurt him or messing with her because the injury wasn't that bad? She had no time to wrestle with insecurity. They needed to get on the road.

"You're not dying on my watch." Grace shut the door, careful to make sure she didn't do worse damage.

~~~

The throbbing continued in Seth's foot. It felt like a lumberjack was taking a mallet to it over and over, sending shivers up his spine. Who knew his body could hurt this badly?

Grace did well getting them to the emergency room entrance with the GPS, considering the blinding rain the entire way there. Once she pulled into the drive, she asked for a wheelchair and rolled him in, then parked the truck.

Two minutes later, she'd jogged back to him. Despite his

pain, he drank in the sight of her, damp hair clinging to her cheeks and forehead. Oh, and those huge blue eyes. She disappeared behind the wheelchair and pushed him forward. Inside, a friendly police officer greeted them. Even with a recent surge of flu in the community, no one else was around. They checked in and waited in the freezing cold area. More shivers ran down his arms.

"You're shaking." Worry furrowed Grace's brows. "You might be going into shock."

Was he? How would he know?

"I'll get help. Be right back." She squeezed his hand and stepped away. If he had to be at a hospital, at least having someone with him made the experience tolerable.

She returned with a nurse beside her. "Here we are." Her mouth twisted with concern.

The nurse looked him over and checked his pulse. "We'll get you into an exam room and give you something for the pain right away."

"Should I go with you or wait here?" Grace caught her lip between her teeth. "I don't want to be in your personal business."

"There's nothing secretive about my foot, now that you've seen my need for a pedicure."

A smile replaced the worried expression. "True."

The nurse pushed him down the hall, one left turn, and they entered a room. An orderly joined them, and while he assisted Seth to the bed covered with blue sheets, the nurse asked one question after another.

"No Ebola. No flu. No smoking. No surgeries." His legs sat horizontally in front of him, while his back rested against the inclined bed. Another tremor racked his frame. "How about a blanket?" He stretched his mouth into the best, totally fake, smile he could conjure.

"We'll get you one. A doctor and a radiology tech will be here shortly." She scooted out the door.

Cautiously, Grace moved to his bedside. Her hand hovered a moment. Then, she reached out and ran soft fingers across Seth's forehead. "I wish she'd hurry so you could feel better."

His breathing shuddered but not from the injury. Warmth radiated through him at her touch. "I don't think I'm acute enough for the stat medical service like they show on TV." He reached up to clasp her hand. "Thanks for being kind to me." Those navy eyes could distract him from almost any pain.

Meeting his gaze, a tender smile floated across Grace's lips. "You're easy to be kind to."

A man wearing blue scrubs wheeled in a large white machine. "I'm here to do your x-ray."

"Interesting. It's portable." Seth took in the unit, temporarily breaking his meditation on the sweet woman beside him.

Grace laughed. "You love the gadgets, don't you?"

"Won't deny it." He shot her a smile while complying with the tech's instructions. "Should she leave the room? Radiation and all?"

The tech gave a half-nod. "It's low exposure, but it couldn't hurt."

"I'll go get a cup of coffee and that blanket they promised." Grace made a quick exit.

Minutes later, she reentered, a coffee aroma trailing her. A blanket lay over one arm while she held a cup in each hand. "I poured two, but I wasn't sure if you could have any. I mean I hope you don't need surgery."

A tall man in a white coat entered behind her. "He deserves a drink. I'm Dr. Hoge." With a firm grip, the doctor shook

Seth's hand. "You've got an impressive couple of breaks. The question is, how good of a patient can you be?" He shot a look at Seth then pivoted toward Grace, as if she might know.

The doctor must've assumed they were a couple. Seth needed to save her the awkwardness. "My options, either way?"

Dr. Hoge's gaze returned to Seth. "If I put you in a cast or boot, I'm going to want you to stay off this foot. No weight bearing for four weeks. The cast provides more protection if you don't think you can be really careful. Either way, if you don't keep your weight off of it, you'll probably need surgery." His brows contracted. "Like pins and rods to keep it in place. Not fun."

"I'll take the cast." He'd be careful. The last thing he wanted was surgery. The words pins and rods, while interesting gadgets, didn't appeal to him when applied to a foot. His foot.

"And you'll need to keep the leg propped up a few days, and after that, use your crutches religiously. No driving." His attention returned to Grace. "He'll need someone to assist him."

She nodded. "I'll watch him like a hawk."

Oh, for goodness' sake. They'd put her on the spot. Once the doctor left, Seth pushed up on his elbows. "Grace, you don't have to be my babysitter."

"I'm actually a fabulous babysitter, but my services won't be free." Her lips twitched. "It'll cost you coffee, internet, and tool-man advice."

Seth's heart puddled. Grace was such a woman of…well, grace.

Chapter 9

"The waiting is always the hardest part." Grace tapped her forehead with the palm of her hand. Why did she say such stupid things? "Except for the pain you're going through. That's worse, of course. Sorry. I'm so crazy."

"Not crazy. The waiting does stink. And the painkiller kicked in, so the ache in my foot is better." Seth's easy smile showed off his straight white teeth.

The cutest little cleft in his chin captured her attention. Though it shouldn't. He'd made it clear that he couldn't be more than friends. She didn't know why, but it wasn't her business. "I'm glad you're feeling better. If you want to go to sleep while we wait for the cast, I can step out and make a couple of phone calls."

"You can do that here. I'm not tired." His heavy eyelids suggested otherwise.

"Actually, most of it can be handled via text." Her fingers flew across her phone. She'd become quite the expert while working for Brooklyn.

"I bet when you type on a keyboard, your hands are a blur." His voice held a tease.

Though she was dying to see the accompanying expression, she didn't dare look at him. "Maybe." She kept her eyes glued to her phone.

When she'd completed the texts, she checked her email. Again. Nothing new. Social media might distract her for another minute or two. One click on the icon, and pictures filled the screen. One particular post hit her like a slap across the face, and she sucked in a breath. "No. They. Are. Not." The words escaped in a pained whisper.

That explained the sudden Caribbean marriage.

"Grace? What's wrong?" Seth sat taller in the bed and leaned toward her.

"It's nothing." But thick tears blurred her vision. The ransacking of her heart was complete. Grace deleted Trevor and Alexa from her friend list. She should've deleted and blocked them a long time ago.

"It's obviously not *nothing*." His voice softened. "You can tell me. I mean, unless you don't want me to know."

"It's not a secret, but I hate to be a downer." And bring up her ex again.

"Because nothing that's happened so far has been a bummer, right?"

Grace couldn't help but laugh. "Right. Keep things upbeat, like waiting on a cast for broken bones."

"Exactly." Lines crinkled the corners of his eyes. "So, talk about anything you want. Including what's upsetting you."

"My ex shared a picture of a sonogram, with his new wife, the one who used to be my best friend." Good. She'd kept her voice strong. Her gaze left her screen to take a peek at Seth.

All signs of his former smile had been erased. In fact, the taut line of his lips and set of his jaw looked as though an enemy had just spit in his face.

Puffing out a quick exhale, Grace smiled hoping to cut the tension. "It's nothing that should really affect me." That ship had sailed when Trevor had left her.

"Did y'all try to have children?" Eyes downcast, he shook his head and held up his palm. "Sorry. None of my business. And I assumed you don't have any, but I could be wrong about

61

that too."

"We didn't. I don't." Her throat clogged with raw emotion. "We met in college, typical story, and we had this five-year plan for after we married." Or maybe Trevor had come up with the plan. "While he finished his master's and built his career, I would work. Then after five years, we'd start trying, and I could stay home with…" She swallowed hard at the thickness in her throat. "You know. Anyway, I guess he still had a plan, just not with me." And that ripped an enormous hole in her self-confidence. What was wrong with her? So wrong that he had to find fulfillment with another woman? Her eyes burned again, despite her attempts to keep her emotions in check.

"Grace." Seth's voice came out husky. "He's an idiot to lose you."

~~~

A ball of intense anger pitted in Seth's gut. Although they'd never met, this Trevor guy sounded like a jerk. And Grace's best friend? Didn't those people realize how blasting their news on social media would humiliate sweet Grace? She deserved better.

Better than Seth Gibbs, too, no doubt. He'd been too focused on his career to pay attention to the nice girls his friends introduced him to in his early twenties. Meeting Selina at a tradeshow had taken him off guard. She'd been more career-minded than he was.

He shook off thoughts of Selina and focused on Grace again. "You wanted to be a stay-at-home mom?"

Despite being rimmed with tears, her navy eyes lit up. "I know not everyone understands that choice, but ever since I was a kid with a baby doll and a kitten playing house, I've always wanted to be a mother, homeschool kids, cook, clean, organize—all that fun stuff."

"You mean you always wanted to *clean?*" Despite the squeezing of his heart, Seth chuckled. "You are a non-conformist."

"You mean misfit weirdo?"

He shook his head. "No way. I like a clean store, a clean house. And I appreciate organization."

"Your garage looked like there was a place for everything, and everything was in its place."

"I think my dad has something to that effect on a plaque at every single store in the country. Or maybe my mom tattooed it on my arm." He lifted his sleeve and pretended to check his bicep. The conversation had its light points, but he might as well plow into the place he'd rather avoid. "How many kids do you want?"

Wistfulness replaced her exuberance, making him wish he'd kept his mouth shut.

"I doubt I'll ever have any, but in my mind, I always thought four would be fun."

"Four?" His heart pinched at the visual that conjured. "Not many families have that many anymore. I have three brothers, and it was fun for me, but I don't know how much fun it was for my mom. We fought constantly. Of course, we always had each other's backs when it came to outsiders."

"That's what families are supposed to be like, I guess."

True, but he'd hidden those thoughts away. "Why not teach school if you like kids that much?"

"I've taught at church and been a substitute teacher, but that didn't feel like my calling. Babysitting or being a nanny for a family—I enjoyed that. I liked one-on-one, playing games, singing, reading stories, baking cookies." Her smile conveyed such joy. "I love doing those things."

Memories of growing up in a family just like the one Grace

described flooded his mind. He missed his brothers and nieces and nephews. He'd pushed them away for too long, but he couldn't seem to muster the strength to be around them.

"What about you?" Grace's gaze fluctuated between sad and hopeful. "How many kids would you want? If all was right with the world, that is?"

Another sucker punch. This one swept the air from his lungs. That dream had been buried someplace deep and untouchable.

Because all wasn't right with his world.

But being with Grace, her bright smile through tears... Funny, he'd always wanted a brood of four, too. Like how he'd grown up.

But that would never happen. He couldn't risk it.

A suffocating silence fell between them like a heavy curtain, blocking out oxygen and light. Grace waited, never pushing. He needed to explain, but his mouth had become paralyzed. Maybe his lungs, too.

"Knock, knock." A man with a thick mustache entered, rolling in supplies. "I'm here to cast your foot."

~~~

Thank the Lord. Grace let out a pent-up breath. Seth was finally getting his cast, and that awkward, crickets-chirping silence had been broken. Guilt clawed at her throat, but for the life of her, she couldn't pin down exactly why. Other than the panic-stricken expression that had taken possession of Seth's face when she'd asked about kids.

Did he think she was going to stop at the Justice of the Peace on the way to his house or something? Get him to be the father of her children?

Though that might be dreamy actually, if he was the man she suspected him to be, capturing him hadn't been her intent.

In fact, he was the one who'd asked *her* how many children she wanted. Of course, maybe he was just being sympathetic since she'd shared about Trevor's social media post. And then she'd turned it into far more than he'd bargained for. She wasn't in Santa Rosa scoping out a man to feel sorry for her. Nor was she here to lasso her next husband-victim. She'd only come to process her emotions. Forgive. Move on. If she made that clear to Seth, maybe he'd quit flipping out on her.

Once the cast was in place, the tech went over the instructions for bathing and all. That brought a rush of heat to Grace's cheeks, but Seth assured them he could manage that part alone.

"Now for the crutches." The physical therapist unwrapped the end that fit under the arms. "Have you ever used these bad boys?"

"Never. I've been injury-free my whole life."

Until he met me. The negative thought burst into Grace's mind, but she tried to squash it. She hadn't tripped him. Surely her gracelessness wasn't infectious.

The therapist explained the proper way to carry the weight on the hands instead of the armpits. He had Seth come to his feet to measure the height and take a few steps using the crutches.

Paperwork arrived during the process, and before long, they were on the way to the house.

Seth sat in the truck's backseat again and closed his eyes. Whether he was sleeping or not, she didn't know, but the ride was quiet until they reached the driveway.

Mac ran from next door, arms flapping, as they drove in.

"Oh my, he's excited. And he'll probably call me *little lady* again." Grace spoke out loud, forgetting about Seth.

A laugh came from the rear seat. "He always calls me

buddy."

"While we were at the hospital, I sent a short text explaining that you'd fallen. Looks like he cares about his *buddy*." Smiling, Grace put the truck in park and let her window down.

"Little lady, I've been worried sick about you and my buddy. What happened?" Mac removed his cap and peered into the truck.

Sitting up, Seth waved. "I'm good. Just have my foot in a cast for a while. Thanks."

That news seemed to relieve the plumber. "Whew. I know a break like that hurt, but I'm glad that's the worst of it." He bounced up and down like a bobblehead. "We're going to take real good care of you. Don't you worry."

Once Mac left, Grace watched Seth's first attempts on the crutches, and she fought the urge to walk behind him to make sure he didn't fall. Squashing her overprotective instincts would be a battle over the coming days if she was going to help him out. He wouldn't want to be babied.

Seth paused and made eye contact with her, churning up warmth and unfathomable emotion, considering the short period she'd known him. "You've truly been a godsend, Grace. Thank you."

Her overprotective nature might not be the only thing she had to battle. Her heart seemed to be preparing for a fight, as well.

Chapter 10

Everywhere Grace went, there was Seth. All afternoon. Even when she left him resting on the couch while she crossed to and fro to check on Brooklyn's house, the man's presence seemed to linger on her skin, her heart, her mind. Something between scorching flames and cool gentle waves on a summer day, which totally made no sense, but all she knew was that every moment away from him, she missed him.

Which also made no sense.

"Miss Grace? Did you settle on a plan?" Mac's voice reminded her there were decisions to be made.

Why couldn't Brooklyn pick out her own toilet, tile, knobs, and faucets for the guest bathroom? She'd already chosen for the kitchen, and the woman had exquisite taste, plus a decorator on speed dial. But her boss had insisted Grace could make these decisions with Seth's help. And they could *wait* until he felt up to it. "No rush," Brooklyn had stated. The words had been followed by more of those uncharacteristic giggles.

"I'll call you as soon as I have a plan put together, Mac."

"Yes, ma'am. These things take time." Mac removed his hat and pushed over the thin strip of graying hair remaining on his head. "My wife wants to bring ribs and baked beans over for y'all to have for supper. You've had a long day."

"How sweet, but…" Grace shook her head and waved him off. "She doesn't have to go to any trouble. I can—"

"No trouble at all. Should be here any minute. Pretty good cook, too, in my humble opinion." His head dipped, and he replaced the hat.

"Thank you, then. I'll wait for her at Seth's." No sense having to lug it over.

Grace gathered supplies at Brooklyn's, then crossed the yards and let herself into Seth's back door. The rain had finally let up, and long shadows fell across the room.

Grace's heart skipped when she spotted an empty couch. She dropped her load on a table near the door. "Where did he go?" Anxiety coursed through her, and she headed toward the bedroom. "Seth?"

"Right here." Seth stood near the master bath door, crutches under his arms, a sleepy smile pressing in that little dimple on his chin.

"Why are you up?" Her hands popped to her hips.

"I wanted to brush my teeth."

"I could've brought everything to you for that."

"Um." His smile turned sheepish. "Nature called."

"Oh." Her cheeks burned, and she crossed her arms. "You made it okay? I mean…" What did she mean? Her gaze returned to the downturned picture frame beside the bed. The position of the photo was substantially closer to the edge than when they'd left for the hospital. Was he thinking of his ex-wife? Wishing she were here instead?

"You need to lie down and put your foot up." She waved him forward. "I found another icepack next door, and Mac's wife is bringing food."

"Yes, Nurse Nightingale." He took slow, careful steps on the crutches through the house until he reached the couch. "I'd hoped you were going to use your Suzy-Homemaker-Pioneer-Woman skills and cook me dinner, but I guess I'll have to wait."

"Tomorrow is another day." She couldn't stop a smile.

"And I brought a game of Scrabble over if you feel up to it."

"Scrabble?" He eased himself down and lifted his cast onto the ottoman. "I was planning to skunk you in cards, since you do the lying-lip-twitch thing."

"I do not lie. And that's why I brought Scrabble. So I can win." No lips twitching there. All true.

"We'll see about that."

The doorbell chimed, interrupting what definitely felt like flirting. Grace took a deep breath and stepped away. Thank goodness. "Must be Mrs. Strahan. I'll get it."

"Get ready to be called sugar at least a dozen times."

"I am sweet." Looking back, Grace winked, and Seth's face brightened, but also shaded pink.

Apparently she had no impulse control around this man. How in the world would she get through the next few hours with her heart intact, much less survive the next several days?

~~~

A strong current swept through Seth's body like a high voltage shock. The only explanation for the crazy amps could be the tiny motion of Grace's wink.

God, why does she affect me this way when I'm trying my best to stay in the friend zone? He groaned. *Now she has to take care of me, and I can't seem to control one blasted thing about the situation.*

A verse from the daily Bible reading sprung to his mind.

Forget the former things; do not dwell on the past. See, I am doing a new thing.

Forget? His gut tightened. He could never forget Noah.

But maybe he needed to let go. Because dwelling on the past—he was guilty. Still, this verse didn't make sense. Was God doing a new thing? How did Grace fit in?

Voices floated through, Mac and Darlene Strahan's, along with the aroma of pork and spicy barbeque sauce. Seth's stomach rumbled. He'd enjoyed Darlene's cooking in the past, and this was probably going to be pretty tasty.

"Hey, sugar. You poor, poor baby." Mrs. Strahan came near, her brows knitted below her teased, red hair. "I started cooking as soon as I heard. Made my special Mississippi mud pie, too. So good and chocolaty, it'll make you want to kiss your mama. People say 'slap your mama,' but I can't abide that saying." She raised her shoulders, which made her bright purple shirt dotted with colorful butterflies flutter on her small frame. The woman was maybe five feet, and not more than a hundred pounds soaking wet. "I mean, who would ever want to slap their mama?" She hovered over Seth and pinched one of his cheeks. "Not a good boy like you."

"Aw, Darlene. That boy is a grown man who probably doesn't want you babying him." Mac gave his wife a tender smile. "Not too much, anyway."

"I'll baby him if I want to, and you know it." Though she huffed, her red-lipstick-covered lips curled into a playful pout. She kept her attention on Seth. "We tried and tried to have our own children, but that never worked out, so it became my mission to adopt—and spoil—whoever needs me at the time. God has blessed me in bountiful and unexpected ways all these years."

Guilt pricked Seth's heart and burned his eyes. Instead of giving up like he had, this humble woman had used her grief to bless others. Exactly what Seth kept feeling led to do lately, but the situation seemed so confusing. Falling for Grace hadn't been the way he'd expected God to use him. That couldn't be what God intended.

"Oh, sugar." Darlene's hand cupped his cheek. "I didn't mean to bring up... I'm sorry."

"I'm just overwhelmed by your kindness." Seth blinked

back the moisture in his eyes and smiled. "Why don't y'all stay and eat with us?"

"I did make plenty." Darlene ducked her chin, looking unsure.

Grace neared, confusion scrunching her forehead. "Seth, you look like you're in pain. I can call and ask for stronger medicine to be sent to a pharmacy."

"I'm fine. And hungry." He chuckled and made a fake frown. "Fix me a plate, woman. And our company, too."

Relief swept the lines away. "That *is not* the way you speak to your caregiver." A teasing smirk accompanied Grace's eye roll.

"I was playing."

"You better be, buddy. You're just lucky you're injured." Grace's hand popped to her forehead. "Oh, that didn't come out right. I'm sorry you were hurt."

He loved the way she backpedaled when she thought she'd said something wrong. "I'm just lucky you're here."

Once they'd all devoured the ribs and sides, then the chocolate pie of almost sinful delight, the Strahans took their leave. Seth sank against the couch and let his eyes close. The knock of cabinets opening and closing drifted from the kitchen, where Grace buzzed around cleaning. He'd love to be helping her. Or even just watching her.

Finally, footsteps came near.

"Want me to turn out these lights?" Her voice was soft.

"What?" Seth leaned forward and rubbed his palms together. "I'm dying to beat you at Scrabble. Let's do it. Unless you're too tired." He lifted one brow. "Or scared."

"Oh, you're on." She wagged a finger at him. "And don't expect any mercy."

"I wouldn't want it any other way." He gave an evil laugh.

"Three brothers, remember? I don't know anything about mercy."

He studied the smiling, blue-eyed woman across the coffee table from him. He might not know much about mercy, but he couldn't stop wanting to know more about Grace.

Chapter 11

"I don't mind, Seth." Grace would never forgive herself if her neglect forced Seth to require surgery. He'd fallen while trying to help her, after all. "I'll sleep on your couch, at least tonight."

"You don't need to stay. Sometimes I have nightmares, and I talk in my sleep. I'd drive you crazy." Seth shook his head and took a wobbly step or two away from the couch. "I can call you if I need anything."

The painkiller they'd given him had him a bit loopy and unsteady. Another reason she shouldn't leave him alone.

"You can't call me if you're on the floor writhing in pain." She gave him a pleading look. "I won't sleep a wink anyway if I'm across the way. I'll be worried all night. Unless you have a baby monitor or something that would broadcast to Brooklyn's house?"

Something about the way his chin dipped and the way the corners of his mouth turned down made her feel guilty. Yes, she was being pushy. But she'd feel terrible if she left him here alone.

"First you beat me in Scrabble using obscure legislative terms, now you're treating me like a child." One side of his mouth ticked up, and he gave her a mischievous look. "You took the *no mercy* thing seriously. You'd fit right in with my family."

A bit of the guilt evaporated like morning fog under the warmth of his gaze and his teasing words. He was relenting.

Playing along, she touched her hand to her heart. "I used

obscure words? What about that weird hardware term you plugged in to use your Q? I still think that was a proper name and so not eligible." She blew out a huff. "I'm just glad you didn't try to use *fiddlesticks*, your choice word from when you fell."

"Grace, you won." With a teasing scrunch of his nose, he poked a crutch her way and shook it. "You don't have to keep rubbing it in and making fun of me. My dearly departed grandpa said fiddlesticks all the time."

"Sorry." His stance with his waving crutch unnerved her. He could fall. "Please forgive me for picking on you. And can you keep that crutch on the ground?"

He plopped it down and hobbled closer. Too close. His amused sky-blue eyes completely discombobulated her brain and her breathing apparatus. So close, she could make out the tiniest swirls of silver in his irises like thin clouds on the edge of their stratosphere. Despite her paralyzed lungs, in his gaze, she felt—or maybe imagined—suffering and kindness...and perhaps longing...churning in the mix.

"You might be demoted from Nurse Nightingale to Nurse Ratched if you don't watch out."

"My pride can't take another hit, so I better straighten up." Getting demoted by her best friend and husband had robbed her of enough self-confidence.

"I'm kidding." He released his crutch to squeeze her shoulder. "I appreciate your help."

Her pulse drummed in her throat. He was close enough to kiss her again, and his calloused fingers still rested on her shoulder, each one blazing against her skin, sending bursts of energy through her, like a defibrillator bringing her heart to life.

She took a step back. "You're welcome. I...need to go check out some toilets before bedtime." Way to ruin a moment. "For Brooklyn's guest bathroom, of course."

She could've said tile, cabinet doors—anything but toilets. Grace summoned the composure she seemed to have left somewhere on Interstate 285 in Atlanta.

Seth's hearty laugh relieved her tension. "You've come to the right place, then. Hit the motherlode here. I'll show you where the library of catalogs are stored."

She trailed Seth to a linen closet in the hall. Hands still on the crutches, he pointed toward the handle. "Have at it. Plumbing is on the second shelf in alphabetical order by company, but get the two with the round yellow sticker on the spine. You'll find pages tabbed with our favorite choices and the reason why written in the margins."

She turned the knob and opened the door. Taking in the mass of books and the insanely perfect filing system, she gasped. "Wow. Amazing job." When she'd taken over as Brooklyn's assistant, she'd reorganized like mad, but she might've met her match in Seth.

"The other catalogs have the same methodology." Pride shone in his eyes, but he gave a nonchalant shrug. "Too much time on my hands, obviously."

"I can relate." On the difficult evenings after the divorce, she'd thrown herself into her work, creating the most ridiculous extra projects to keep her mind occupied.

"Want me to stay up with you and pick? It'll go quicker, and I can place the order electronically tonight."

"You need your rest. You can check it in the morning." Though she'd much rather have his help.

"I've been lying around since I fell this morning. I'm really not tired."

"If you're sure."

"Little lady, I could talk about remodeling all night." He

performed a nice impression of Mac, pulling a chuckle from Grace.

"That's a few hours longer than I had in mind." She stacked several of the heavy catalogs with the yellow dots marking them in her arms. "After you." She motioned with her head toward the couch. The top book slipped, but she caught it at the last second. "Oh, fiddlesticks! I almost hit your foot."

"But you didn't." His tone was soothing. "Are you making fun of my grandpa's favorite word again?" This time he winked, blasting off bottle rockets in her chest.

"Not deliberately." She nodded toward the couch. "I'll give you a head start to get settled before I lug this over, just to be on the safe side." Maybe one book at a time to cool her scorching cheeks.

An hour later, Seth had guided her through what would be needed, and Grace had a completed list. Every choice had been simple with his expert knowledge and patient explanations. She'd heard projects like this one had people tearing out their hair, but she'd actually had fun. Of course, it was Brooklyn's money they were spending.

"I wish I could help you put these catalogs away." Seth's gaze traveled her face, lingering on her lips. "But I know you won't let me."

Grace swallowed hard at the thickness in her throat. "You'd be correct."

"Are you sure you won't take a room upstairs? That couch can be hard on the back."

"I'm made of rubber and springs, remember?" She forced a smile. "Get some rest, but yell if you need me."

"I'll holler really loud, *sugar*." This time he sounded a lot like Darlene.

"I'm serious, Seth."

"I know. Good night, Grace."

The tenderness of his voice tugged at her emotions. There might not be an easy night's sleep here, either, and not just because she'd be listening for his call.

~~~

Morning light crept in through the windows facing the Gulf. Grace stretched her arms and legs then swung off the couch. The night on the sofa hadn't been bad at all—other than the amazing kiss that kept tiptoeing into her mind. Okay, maybe stomping into her mind. That moment seemed to be a stubborn thought attempting to brand itself front and center. And she needed to erase it.

Grace positioned into a few of the Pilates poses she'd learned. The positions helped her focus, and she often prayed through them. Taking the classes had been another attempt to correct her balance issues. Ballet, barre, Christian yoga, CrossFit...they hadn't alleviated the problem, but she'd enjoyed the exercise. Except for that foray into Zumba, though. She still cringed about that mishap.

Body awake, she made her way to the kitchen to start a pot of coffee. After reading countless health articles before she went to sleep, she'd come up with a list of healing foods for Seth to eat. Now, to figure out what he had in his kitchen and what she'd need to pick up at the store. Stealthily as possible, she opened his cabinets and refrigerator making a list on her phone of the needed items. Mentally, she noted what he had so she could make a healthy breakfast. She'd do her best to look after him. It would be nice to have a guy friend in Atlanta to hang out with when they went back, if nothing else.

~~~

Nine a.m. already? Seth stared at his phone. Despite the broken foot, he'd slept soundly. No nightmares—that he

77

remembered, and Grace hadn't run into the room for anything, so all seemed well. He brushed his teeth and ran his fingers through his hair. The aroma of home-cooking, maybe sausage, led him to the kitchen, taste buds clamoring to find the source.

"I could get used to this." Leaning against his crutches, he took in the spread Grace had going on the stove.

"Oh, I didn't hear you get up." That perky smile met him like a warm embrace. "And I was listening. I hope I didn't wake you."

"I didn't hear a thing, but that mouthwatering smell hit me as soon as I hobbled out of the bedroom. What have we here?"

"After you went to bed, I researched foods that help heal the bones. I hope you don't mind, but I searched your cabinets and refrigerator to see what you had. I made a list for us."

He sure liked the sound of that. *Us.* The two-letter word hammered against his resolve to keep his emotions in check.

As if trying to justify her kitchen takeover, she motioned wildly around the room with a spatula. "I came up with an egg casserole, hash browns, pumpkin-banana-nut muffins, and frozen berries with yogurt."

She set aside the spatula, put on an oven mitt, and opened the stove. A glass dish held egg casserole, which looked to have sausage and maybe green chilies in it, almost capturing his attention as much as the adorable cook.

She pulled the steaming creation out and set it on the stove with the other bowls and pans. Then she smiled and tucked a wayward strand of honey-brown hair behind her ear. Definitely more interesting than the casserole.

"You have a surprisingly well-stocked kitchen."

"I try." Patting his stomach, he attempted to make the food the focal point of the conversation and his attention. "A man's gotta eat. My mom insisted we learn to cook. With four boys, she couldn't keep up with our appetites."

"Wow, I bet she would've been run ragged if she'd tried." Empty plates waited on the countertop, and Grace held one out. Her blue gaze met his. "What will you have?"

Oh, if only things were different.

Warning bells alarmed in his head. He had to stop this fantasy, because nothing had changed. Their paths couldn't converge. "Two helpings of each. Everything looks amazing."

Once she had both dishes served, she insisted he sit at the couch, elevate his foot, and let her bring him a tray. He complied. Most meals, he ate in the living room anyway. Nothing new. Nothing that was about to change.

They'd only taken a couple of bites when the doorbell rang. Grace set aside her food. "Do you think it's Mac?"

Seth swallowed a gulp of the delicious eggs topped with a dab of salsa. "I'm not expecting anyone."

"I'll check it out." She flitted off to answer the door.

Wide-eyed, Grace returned with a woman behind her. Wearing a bright red business suit and three-inch pumps to match, the attractive blond real estate agent stood out like a beacon in the room of mostly cool, natural colors.

He hadn't seen that one coming. Seth pressed three fingers to his forehead. "Susan, I forgot about our meeting." He never expected her to show up at his house. He didn't remember giving her his address when they'd met at the architectural advisory meeting, but a real estate agent could have easily searched it out.

"I was worried you'd forgotten, so I decided to come find you." A flirty gaze lifted her sculptured brows. "I'm sorry you broke your foot. Anything I can do?"

"Grace is taking good care of me." He directed a smile Grace's way. The last thing he wanted was to make her feel uncomfortable after everything he'd put her through already.

"I see." Susan's voice flattened. She'd been pretty direct in both her real estate sales attempts and her interest in him beyond selling a storefront.

Keeping his attention on Grace, he tried to explain. "I've been giving thought to opening and managing a small specialty hardware shop over near the grocery store, and Susan had a property coming open. I completely forgot I had an appointment to look at the space today."

Chin tilted, Grace met his gaze head on, the intensity driving a nail into his conscience. "You don't ever plan to live in Atlanta again?"

"It's just an idea I've been toying with." The millionth stupid thing he'd said since meeting Grace. "I mean..."

"I'll give you two some privacy." Grabbing her plate, she took off toward the kitchen.

Chapter 12

Just an idea I've been toying with.

Seth's words ran through Grace's mind while she kept herself busy in the kitchen. The water rushing over the dishes drowned out the content of Seth and Susan's conversation in the other room.

Why did she care if he wanted to make his home in Santa Rosa? They barely knew each other.

Yet, for some reason, the thought still pinched... *toyed with* her emotions. If he intended to return to Atlanta, there was a chance they could hang out, at least. But if he built a new business here, she'd probably never see him again after she left. It wasn't as if Brooklyn had ever invited her down before. And pretty Susan-the-real-estate-agent had an empty ring finger and looked to be interested in more than leasing a retail space.

Looked? Yeah, that was a total understatement. The woman stalked the man's home when a simple text would have done the job just fine. She wasn't looking. She was hunting.

A door clattered as it shut, and Grace cut off the water.

"Grace?" Seth's voice called from the couch.

She took quick steps to check on him. "Is your friend gone?"

"Yes." His chin dipped as he peered up at her. "I hate that the timing interrupted our breakfast. Everything was wonderful, but did you get to enjoy any of it?"

"I did." Though she'd eaten alone in the kitchen, she couldn't help but be a little proud of how well the food had

81

turned out. Cooking for one wasn't as fulfilling as preparing a meal to share. Having someone appreciate the results made the effort worthwhile.

"Do you need to go next door for a shower or to check on the house? I promise to be good if you want to take a break."

Man code for *he wanted a break*. She probably should've left when she'd found Susan at the door, but the woman's arrival had thrown her off-kilter. More off-kilter than she already was. "I do need to tell Mac about the orders we made and when the deliveries should arrive." She needed a shower, too. "I'll get out of your hair for a while. Call me if you need anything."

"You're not in my hair, but you're welcome to brush it if it's sticking up." A mischievous look twinkled in his eyes, hurling her emotions into a seesaw. The up and down was dizzying. "And I fully expect you to come back to feed me and give me a do-over in Scrabble."

"Another do-over?"

"I seem to need a heap of grace." His smile couldn't become any more charming.

Warmth heated her whole face, and a giggle slipped past her lips. "Since you put it that way, I'll go take care of business and return ready for a battle." Still smiling, she slipped through the door.

Once she was outside, she scolded herself. She shouldn't enjoy his company so much. He wouldn't be in her life for long. She was only lobbing her heart up to be smashed once again.

Really, she should plan for a future all on her own. The income she earned as Brooklyn's assistant was good, but she'd reached the ceiling there. She'd made plenty of connections while arranging appointments for her boss, developing important documents, attending luncheons with powerful people. Perhaps she could move into a position at the Capitol or even become a lobbyist herself for the right issues.

Outside, Mac unloaded two Christmas trees from the bed of his truck, each measuring around five feet. He waved when he spotted her. "Hey, Miss Grace. The wife wanted me to deliver some Christmas spirit to you and Mr. Gibbs. I'll set these blue spruces in their stands, and you let me know if you don't have decorations. She'll pick up whatever you need."

"How sweet. Thank you. I'm not sure what Brooklyn has, or Seth, either. Let me get my purse, and I'll pay you."

"It wouldn't be a gift if you did that." A grin split his beard-stubbled face. "Merry Christmas."

The kindness of this couple overwhelmed her. Grace's throat thickened. Never in her years of church attendance had she gone to such lengths to reach out to those around her. In fact, she often, in her busyness, failed to pay attention. Mac and Darlene set a great example she wouldn't forget.

~~~

Seth pressed the remote to turn on the stereo system and found a station playing Christmas music while Grace sorted through the boxes of decorations Mac had retrieved from the attic. Merriment merged with dread and rolled over Seth like shifting tides. Three years had passed since he'd thought of decorating for the holidays.

Ornament after ornament, Grace smiled and asked if there'd been a story about the purchase of that particular piece before hanging it on the tree, unfolding memories he'd kept stored away. His grandmother had given everyone in the family an ornament each year. Each one commemorating an event or vacation. Both his grandparents had been such special people, taking him and his brothers fishing and boating, teaching them about carpentry and nature. He sure missed them.

"Oh, what a cute baby." She held up a hand-painted ceramic frame that read, 'Noah's First Christmas.'

Chills prickled him. Silent screams of grief rushed through Seth's throat, stilling his breath as he glimpsed the precious face of his son. That baby smile, one chubby hand raised, fingers splayed. Those fingers that would curl around Seth's thumb, holding him. A burn stung his eyes—all a stark reminder of the reason he'd left the boxes in the attic. Selina had packed them just two months before they'd lost Noah. Haunted by the memories, he'd fought to pick himself up for the past three years, broken piece by broken piece, without much success.

"Seth?" Grace gently set the ornament on the coffee table and crossed the room to kneel at his side. "Are you okay?"

Tears choked him as he tried to drag his gaze away from the photo. How tremendously innocent. How horribly unfair. He forced himself to breathe. As much as he didn't want to, maybe it was time to open up.

"There's more to my story than a divorce."

Chapter 13

Tears streamed down Seth's face, and his shoulders heaved with the force of his sobs.

Grace stilled on her knees beside him, waiting. Only once had she seen a man she knew cry. She could still remember her father's chest shaking as he tried to gain control before her grandmother's funeral. The memory sparked her own tears.

Seth's fingers swiped across his cheekbones. "Sorry." He cleared his throat. "I don't mean to diminish your pain, because divorce is like a death. It's just, my own marriage broke up after our son, Noah, passed away, not too long after that photo was taken."

"Oh, Seth. I'm so sorry." Understanding struck her, all the pieces falling in place about his strange behavior, wrenching her heart. What a nightmare he must've lived through. "There are no words... I can't imagine the grief after a loss like that."

"Yeah, when we talked about bad things to say after a divorce, I could've added a whole list of things not to say when a child dies." A bitter laugh slipped through his lips. "'He's in a better place. He's home. It was his time. God knows what He's doing... You can have another child.'" Seth's voice broke, but he continued. "None of those words made sense. I didn't want it to be *Noah's time* or for him to *go home*. I wanted him in *our home*." Frustration laced his wild gestures. "And how could having another child ever replace our son? That's like saying, 'Sorry your wife died, but you can get another one.'" His head dropped in his palms, and he massaged his forehead.

"Honestly, God may know what He's doing, but I don't."

"I'm sorry," she repeated in a whisper and rested a hand on his. "I can pack this stuff up. We don't have to talk about it."

"What I want seems to be in direct opposition to where God's casting me." He inhaled a breath that appeared to fill his shoulders. "But I'm clinging to my belief that He is good, and He loves me, no matter how badly my heart's been broken."

"He is, and He does."

"I know." His voice was quiet...solemn. "Will you hang the picture on the tree for me? Someplace on the front where I can see Noah."

"If you're sure." Hesitant, she picked up the ornament, moved to the tree, and hooked it over a branch at eye level. The sweet face saturated Grace's heart with a minuscule taste of Seth's pain. "How's that?"

"Perfect." Though his blue eyes were glassy, he offered a shaky smile. "He was amazing."

She turned her gaze to study the picture. A little bald head with huge blue eyes looked up at her. "He is." She caught her lip under her teeth for a moment, debating, choosing her next words. "Can I ask what happened? If you don't want to discuss it, that's okay."

He gave a slow nod, and his eyes darted to another place and time. "Selina had a cold, so I put Noah to bed that night. He usually still took a bottle around four, and I got up and warmed the formula. When I went in..." He stared at his hands in front of him. "I followed every rule—laid him on his back, made sure there was nothing in the crib. But still he..."

A sharp burn slid across her chest, a jagged ache for the pain Seth had gone through—was still going through—losing a child to SIDS. She sat beside him and took his rough hand in hers. "What happened wasn't your fault. You have to know that."

"I've tried to convince myself. My family has tried to convince me. But Selina had to lay the blame somewhere. On me."

"She was wrong. Your family is right."

"The thing is, I can't figure out how to move forward. I stepped out in faith when I took you to dinner, then when I heard that baby crying..."

"Seth, the thing about stepping out or moving forward—and I know this better than most—is that sometimes you fall, but you get up and dust yourself off. You try again."

"I want to." His Adam's apple bobbed with a hard swallow. "Part of my reason for looking at the property here was to start over."

Something didn't sound right about the logic. "What was the other part of staying here instead of going back to Atlanta?"

His gaze dropped, his forehead creasing. "Being there hurts too much. I bought Selina's share of our house, hired someone to keep it up, and left. All my brothers...they have healthy babies, which I'm thrilled about, but my family is tight knit. Or was." He shook his head. "Being with them is too hard."

So he'd been avoiding. Grace held in a sigh, her heart overflowing with sympathy for Seth. How easy it would've been to fall into that trap. Hanging out with her married friends had hurt, at first, but she'd pushed on. Sure, sometimes situations became awkward, making her feel like a third wheel, but she refused to let despair win. "You can't just hide away here when you have people who love and miss you—and a huge thriving business. What about grief counseling or support groups?"

Seth worked his jaw. He still dodged looking her way. "If you'll excuse me, I think I'll take a nap." He reached for his crutches, but she caught his hand.

"I'm sorry. I overstepped." She'd pushed too hard and strained their tenuous relationship. "We don't have to discuss this again."

He let his shoulders settle into the couch, though his lips remained tight. "I do have some work on the computer that needs my attention. Would you mind bringing my laptop from my bedroom?"

"Sure." She rose and made her way down the hall. He needed a moment, and she'd give it to him. Actually, he'd had three years, but he still seemed to be treading in the depths of despair. Nothing she could say would likely make a difference, but she'd pray earnestly for God to move in Seth's life.

In the bedroom, she scanned the dresser. The laptop rested on a lap pad, and she gathered it all in her arms. Her eyes roamed to the downturned picture on the nightstand, and she took slow steps toward it. Would he be angry if she peeked? More upset than she'd already made him? For some reason, she had to see.

Her fingers hesitated, hovering over the frame, but she finally flipped the picture over. A smiling baby lay in Seth's arms. She gasped at the precious vision. Seth's entire countenance glowed as he gazed at his son. The joy of the scene was palpable.

Tears pressed against Grace's lids. No wonder he was so broken.

Chapter 14

Three weeks had passed too quickly. Out on the deck, a cool breeze swept over Seth. He leaned forward on the chaise lounge to better take in the last of the magenta sunset. Beside him, Grace snapped pictures on her phone, like she'd done every single night. The woman found joy in creation's treasures, and Seth found joy watching the glow on her face...the way her eyes lit up when she discovered a sand dollar or a shell or that one tiny piece of sea glass. Every sunrise or bird or jumping fish. Oh, and dolphins. Grace often ran to the beach and cheered for them when they played nearby. She only fell a few times and always bounced back to her feet. Maybe she was like Tigger.

But despite the fact she'd come to recoup, she'd worked furiously. For her administrative position, she made phone calls and maintained online reports, then she checked the remodeling progress several times a day. She still found time to cook healthy meals and had actually learned to play a mean hand of Rook. They'd laughed, watched church online together, and enjoyed each other's company more than he'd imagined possible. And she'd completely dropped the subjects of grief and children, avoiding the whole touchy issue like he'd wanted.

Was that what he still wanted?

Talking about his son hurt, but he'd grown accustomed to seeing that little face smiling from the frame on the Christmas tree. He'd even kept the picture on his nightstand upright.

Perhaps he could heal, find a new normal, and return to Atlanta. But still, if he was able to move forward, he couldn't imagine ever fathering another child—the terror of the responsibility for another life was just too immense.

The shades of pink spreading across the clouds transformed into a blazing orange before the enormous ball sank into the horizon, leaving a deep lavender sky that was quickly darkening. The days had shortened as Christmas neared.

"Thank you, God. Your mercies are new every day." Beside him, Grace applauded heavenward, and then pivoted Seth's way. "Isn't He wonderful?"

Forcing a swallow, Seth met her gaze. "He is. I'd forgotten how much until you fell—quite literally—into my life." He managed a smile. "Thank you, Grace."

Her face pinked, and her chin took a shy dip. "I've enjoyed our time together."

The unspoken deadline loomed between them. Maybe he would go back to Atlanta, but he'd still have to explain why they could only be friends. The bloom on her cheeks and the deep blue eyes waited for his response.

Why ruin a perfect moment, though? "I've enjoyed getting to spend time with you, too. More than you know. And hey, only two days until Christmas. Would you mind driving me down the road to shop for a few gifts? There's a nice outfitters store and several boutiques we could hobble into."

Scanning his cast, her lips pursed into a worried, but adorable, pooch.

"I'll be careful." He motioned toward his leg. "I've followed the rules so far, and we don't have to stay long...unless you want to grab dinner while we're out." Memories of their first and last attempt at eating out rushed over him, the pleasurable and painful colliding. But they'd eaten together on trays for weeks with no awkward moments. Couldn't they try going out once more? As friends?

~ ~ ~

Grace's breath caught. What should she do? Anxiety about Seth on crutches in a Christmas shopping rush competed with the worry over her growing feelings for him. Neither of those scenarios seemed likely to leave them unscathed, especially the latter.

Seth had already pushed to a stand. "Don't you need to buy a few gifts?"

She'd ordered most of what she needed online, had them gift-wrapped and delivered not long after Thanksgiving, but she would like to buy Mac and Darlene something. They'd been so kind. And maybe something for Seth would be appropriate. They'd hung out every day since her arrival. Would Christmas be any different?

"Come on, Grace." His pleading smile might be her undoing. "We can take my truck. It needs to be cranked since it's been sitting."

"Sure. Let's live dangerously. I'll grab my purse." Even as she agreed, she worried she'd live to regret the outing.

"I'll meet you at the truck with my wallet and keys."

In the garage, Grace pressed the button to open the automatic door and then scanned the shelves on the far wall. At least a dozen sculptures of coastal animals stood there— fish and birds and a crab—created from all kinds of old metal, from screws to faucets to doorknobs. Five birdhouses sat on the shelf above, made from what appeared to be mostly driftwood and seashells. Were these gifts Seth had ordered and not yet wrapped? They were so unique.

"I'm ready, James." Seth's voice still warmed her as it had

91

that first day.

"James?" She turned to face him.

"Like a chauffeur. My grandma used to say that."

"Oh, okay, Miss Daisy. You and your grandparents must've been close."

"We were."

Had he been avoiding them too, or had they passed on? No way was she bringing up more delicate subjects. "It looks like you've already been shopping." She pointed at the creations. "I love the artwork. Where can I buy some for my family? My mom would go crazy over the birdhouse. I'd like one, too."

His mouth curled into a sheepish grin. "Have whatever you want. I made them."

"You?" More admiration bloomed for this man. "They're amazing."

"I've been itching to use my saw and welding tools, but I thought I might get in trouble with my sitter-friend."

Interesting, and somewhat disappointing, description he had for her. "Yes. You would." She pivoted back and neared the sculptures to get a closer view, ran her fingers over a larger one, a heron. Some sort of long needle-nose pliers formed a beak, and the legs were formed from thin metal rods. The body consisted of so many shapes and textures she wasn't sure yet what all he'd used. Despite the harsh materials, the bird appeared graceful. But the birdhouses really attracted her—the delicate shells and driftwood.

"Y'all heading out and about?" Mac had slipped up on them and stood in the driveway.

"Hey." Grace waved him in. "He's convinced me to take him shopping. Have you seen Seth's works of art?" She pointed to the shelves.

Mac neared, bringing the scent of outdoors and hard work with him. He studied the artwork closely. "I knew he recycled, but I had no idea he was an artist." He let out a husky laugh. "Are the eyes on that crab the old faucet handles I gave you?"

"They are." Seth's voice held an edge of hesitancy, as if waiting for approval.

"Isn't that something?" Grinning, Mac turned and placed a hand on Seth's shoulder. "You've taken trash and dead wood and the remains of sea creatures to make something really special. Your pretty work here reminds me of how the Lord can take our garbage and pain, then recycle that chaos into something beautiful."

Grace couldn't help but squeeze the plumber into a tight hug. "Mac, you might be one of the smartest men I've ever met."

Chapter 15

Grace admired the thousands of white Christmas lights illuminating the community square while they waited outside for a table at the cafe. The temps hovered in the low sixties, making for a nice foray around the quaint town. She'd found the presents she needed at the upscale gift stores—a chunky pearl-and-bead necklace for Darlene and a fishing cap for Mac. Nothing seemed right for Seth, though.

The words the old plumber had spoken stayed with her the rest of the evening. If only Seth would believe his brokenness could be recycled into something beautiful when laid in God's hands.

"Hey, they're paging us." Seth's fingers brushed her arm, summoning the usual tingles that accompanied his touch.

"Nice. My stomach was just beginning to complain." She tried and failed to keep her focus on the surroundings and not his incredible eyes.

"We can't have that." Leaning on his crutches, he motioned her ahead of him. "Ladies first."

After inspecting the two steps leading onto the restaurant's deck, Grace looked back at him. "You go ahead."

"Are you going to catch me if I fall?" His smile exhibited a quirk of sarcasm but was still cute.

For about the hundredth time tonight, his gaze whipped up another swarm of butterflies in her midsection that refused to be grounded. "I would give it my best shot."

"I've got the hang of the crutches."

"Fine." Still glued to the vision of him, she turned toward the restaurant entrance and took a step. Her shoe wedged between two boards, and she lurched forward. She caught herself with both arms on the decking. "Oops." Why was it always when she was going up a set of stairs?

"Grace, are you okay?" Seth's crutches clattered to the ground, and he bent to touch her shoulder.

Releasing a trapped breath, she stood, careful not to bump him. "You shouldn't put weight on that cast. I'm still fine, as always."

He straightened, but hobbled one step closer, so close, his breath warmed her cheek. "That you are." His fingers traced the contours of her face, energy pulsing through the caress. His gaze intensified, and his lips brushed hers, slowly, gently, but electrifying.

Her heart seemed to combust, and she responded by drinking him in, pulling closer, running her fingers through his hair. She soaked in the scent of him, woodsy and fresh as cut pine and salt air. Three weeks' worth of pent-up emotion and attraction and affection welled up inside her and permeated the moment. She didn't care a whit about the public display. Apparently, neither did he, because he only deepened the kiss.

"Seth, party of two. Last call." A woman's voice carried from the restaurant entrance.

Seth broke the contact between their lips. One hand remained on Grace's cheek, the other waved at the hostess. "We're coming. We just fell along the way."

"Do you need help?" The woman inched farther out the door.

"None you can provide." Shaking his head, he bent to gather his crutches.

"Take your time. I'll hold the table." She gave an

understanding smile and then reentered the restaurant.

Seth seemed to take her at her word. He gazed into Grace's eyes. "What is it with you and me and restaurants?" His chuckling scoff floated in the gentle breeze. "I mean, we've eaten together for almost a month at the house and…"

Grace's heart galloped. She stepped back and wrapped her arms around herself. What had she been thinking, laying a kiss like that on Seth?

Oh, right. She hadn't been thinking. But *he'd* started the whole thing. Again. "I know you just want to be friends." Moisture collected on her lashes, and she blinked to try and control her sappy self.

"Grace…" His earnest gaze locked on her and wouldn't let go. "Friends is obviously not what I want. But getting involved romantically wouldn't be fair to you in the long run. I can't waste your time or hurt you that way." His expression tensed, and he shook his head. "I can't give you the life you want."

Confusion fogged her mind. What was he saying? "How do you know what I'd want?"

"You want children." He shook his head.

The three simple words tainted the air between them, but why? "And you can't father more?"

"I won't." A muscle in his jaw ticked as he tore his gaze away. "I won't be responsible for another child. I won't go through that pain again. It's just too much. Too hard."

"But…" She needed to be careful how she worded this. If only he would listen… "What happened to Noah wasn't your fault. And just because a tragedy happened once doesn't mean a tragedy like that will happen again."

He looked back at her, a hint of hopeless longing glistening through his resolve. "My grandma said she had a younger brother who died of what they called crib death. What if the condition's genetic?"

"You said your brothers have children?" She blurted the statement then held her breath, regretting her desperate words.

His gaze shifted to his feet, his furrowed brows hooding his face. "I won't take that chance."

~~~

Even though Seth meant the words he'd said, hearing them out loud shattered him anew. Even though he'd meant to save them both more pain, seeing Grace blink away tears broke his heart more than he'd imagined. Even though he believed his choice was best for Grace and for himself, doubt pounded against his determination.

No. He had to allow Grace the opportunity to be the wife and mother she was meant to be—with a man who was whole and unbroken.

She turned her attention to the ground, and shadows veiled her expression. "We better go inside before we lose our chance at a table."

"Okay." No other response came to mind. He pushed his weight against the blasted crutches and limped forward. He'd gotten to know Grace well enough to see how much he was causing her to suffer, but he couldn't play games. Of course, they'd both been playing pretend for three weeks. Pretending they weren't falling for each other. Pretending they weren't both in a ship full of holes in the middle of the Gulf. And it was his fault. He should've stayed in his house that first day. Grace was recovering from one idiotic man's actions already. He'd made things worse.

For once, being seated between a boisterous office party and the two-man band's speaker turned out to be a good thing. Seth scarfed down his dinner and held up one finger to signal the waiter to bring the check. The noise level had effectively drowned out any possibility for conversation between him and Grace.

Grace slid out her chair as soon as the bill had been paid. Her food had barely been touched. The waiter insisted on boxing her salmon and mashed potatoes. Silently, they walked down the boardwalk and through the packed parking lot.

In the truck, Seth caught her hand before she shifted into reverse. "I'm sorry. All I wanted from that first day on the beach was to cheer you up." He gave a mirthless chuckle. "I've blown that one out of the water."

"It is what it is." Her gaze flitted around the windshield, looking anywhere but his way. "I want children. You don't." Shaking her head, she shrugged. "We just met, anyway. It's not like we…" She didn't finish, but he knew what she was thinking and why she'd stopped. Because despite their best efforts—desperate efforts—they'd fallen for each other.

Chapter 16

Seth released Grace's hand and let his own drop to his thigh. Silence filled the truck's cab, so he flicked on the radio. Christmas tunes blared, sounding much too joyful. He turned the volume to barely audible.

The rest of the short drive dragged on. The tension buzzing his entire body had his good leg bouncing.

Finally, they reached the driveway, and Grace slowed. A silver van had parked on the right side. Seth's heart surged, breaking a new speed record.

"Expecting another real estate agent?" Grace glanced his direction for a second, her tone flat.

If only. "It's one of my younger brothers."

"Oh, goodness. I would've made sure the guestrooms were prepared and the furniture was dusted if you'd told me."

"I didn't know." Between the two lawns, Mac and Darlene stood smiling and talking with Cam and his wife, Misty. Their three-year-old daughter, Evie, held her father's hand, and in Misty's arms lay their latest addition—three-month-old Jonathan.

"I can't believe he'd just show up like this. With his kids." His limbs constricted, and his chest clamped against his abs.

"You can do this, Seth. Don't shut out your family." The garage door rose when Grace pressed the remote. She parked then swiveled his way, studying him.

"I talk to Cam every day. We went deep-sea fishing last summer, golfed a couple of times."

"Did you see his family?"

Okay, no. Seth shook his head. He'd seen Misty occasionally, but not Evie or Jonathan, except for the pictures and updates they periodically sent in a group email.

The whole herd made their way to the garage, ready to pounce when Seth exited.

"What happened to you?" Misty's mouth fell open, but she kept her distance with the swaddled baby in her arms.

Still holding Evie's hand, Cam headed straight for him. "Why didn't you tell us you were on crutches, bro? A cast means you broke something."

Every muscle in Seth's body locked up. "I'm fine." He shifted his gaze to Grace. "I've had a friend helping me." Maybe curiosity would turn the attention her way.

"Oh, hey. Sorry to be rude." Cam made introductions, but his attention routed around to Seth. "I knew God was leading us to come here for Christmas for a reason."

"Christmas here?"

"Yep." His brother gave Seth's shoulder a firm squeeze. "We're not leaving you down here alone again. We're gonna do this."

"We?" Surely not everyone.

"The whole gang. The rest will arrive tomorrow."

Mac and Darlene both laughed. "We were coming to invite you and Grace over for Christmas lunch, but sounds like you'll have a full house."

"It was nice meeting everyone." Grace edged toward the driveway, waved, and disappeared around the corner.

He wanted to call her back, but he had to let her go. Today had probably been the last time she'd come to his house. A thousand *if onlys* pounded into his mind, but like Grace had said, *It is what it is.*

~~~

Grace had finally gotten an answer to who Seth Gibbs was. And why they'd never be together. Tears streamed down Grace's cheeks. Continuing dinner at the restaurant after the blow had been torture. Coming to Santa Rosa had been a mistake. Through the whole mess with Alexa and Trevor, she'd never run. She'd plowed through her work and carried on with life.

Maybe she'd pack up tonight. Go home in the morning. Seth's family could take care of him now. Mac was an honest man and could make sure the rest of the work was completed. At the door, she punched in the code. Her parents' flight had already taken them to spend Christmas with her sister in Indianapolis, but she had friends in Atlanta. Someone would let her hang out for the holiday.

"Sweetie, wait." Darlene's voice caught her before she entered the beach house.

Swiping at her wet cheeks, Grace stopped. She hated to be caught blubbering like a baby.

Darlene rubbed Grace's back. "What's wrong, sugar?"

A humiliating sob escaped, and Grace sniffled in a vain attempt to regain control. "I'm just emotional. I'll be fine."

"You can still spend Christmas with us if you want to. We'd love to have you. It's hard being away from family."

All she managed was a nod and a squeaked out, "Thank you."

The petite woman pulled Grace into a fierce hug. "God brought you here for a reason. He's at work, I just know it."

Grace pulled away to look into Darlene's face. "Why would you say that?"

"Honey, I've been praying something or someone would bring that boy outta his house for three years."

"You knew about his son Noah?"

"We've known Seth's family for years. His grandparents had one of the original cottages down the road. Noah and Evelyn Gibbs. Good, solid people."

Aww. Seth's son had been named after his grandpa. "What happened to them?"

"Evelyn died from pneumonia one winter after a bout with the flu. Two months later, Noah died in his sleep. A heart attack, they said. I never saw a couple more in love. Sometimes when people are together that long, they do seem to become one."

"Like you and Mac?"

"We've had our tough times, but we never gave up on each other." A sheen covered Darlene's eyes. "Infertility, heartbreaking adoption attempts that never panned out. They shattered my heart, and I got real low."

"That had to have been difficult. No one can blame you."

"I guess I had a right to be disappointed. But at some point, I had to let God gently pick me up, set me on my feet, and trust that He had another plan for Mac and me." A shaky smile lifted her countenance. "And He's filled our lives with blessing on top of blessing."

"I may come celebrate with y'all on Christmas. I'll let you know." Oh, that she could absorb some of that trust Darlene had found.

"Or you could keep working with God on that boy next door." Darlene winked and left Grace alone with her deliberations.

Chapter 17

Battling urges assailed Seth. One to throw away his crutches and run to catch Grace. The other to hop in the truck and escape his brother's family and all the memories they shoveled to the surface. Deep down, he knew he couldn't—shouldn't—stay away from love or family forever. He looked into Evie's big blue eyes framed with strawberry blond curls and tried to maintain his composure. Evelyn and Noah had been born the same year, only a month apart. Their names had been chosen to honor their grandparents. And no matter how hard he'd tried to understand why Noah was gone, his death never made sense. Would Noah have looked like her? Would they have reached the milestones around the same time? Walking, talking, smearing birthday cake all over their faces?

"Are you my uncle? You look like my daddy." Evie's small voice chattered, and her fingers caught his wrist.

This sweet child couldn't help that every time he saw her, sadness overtook him for what might've been. Thank the Lord, she'd thrived.

"I am your uncle." He forced his lips to smile despite the burn in his eyes and twist of his heart.

"Can we play in your house?"

God, help me. "Sure, baby. Come in."

Misty was at his side in an instant, hugging him. "We love you, Seth."

A vise tightened around his throat. "I know. I love y'all, too."

Cam directed his gaze to his wife. "You want to take the kids in and get them bathed while Seth and I unload?"

Obviously, his brother planned to give him a pep talk while gathering the bags and baby equipment, because being on crutches limited the amount of unloading he'd contribute to. "Grace washed a load of towels this afternoon, so if you need more, they're folded in the laundry room."

Misty's brows spiked. "This Grace sounds fascinating. I expect to hear more once these two are asleep."

Then he'd get another *talk* from Misty. "We'll see."

"Yes, we will." She shot him a determined look. "Let's go, Evie. Daddy and Uncle Seth will come in a few minutes." They disappeared inside the house, and the door clicked shut.

Seth took a deep breath, trying to gain control of the cyclone spiraling inside him.

"Grace, huh?" Cam's voice intruded into the storm. "What's the story?"

Explaining their messed-up relationship might be the nail in his coffin. "Complicated."

"The short version, then."

"We met. We really like each other. She wants kids. I don't. The end." He swallowed against the lump strangling him. "As of right before y'all got here."

"No. You. Didn't." His brother's forehead scrunched into a scowl, and a familiar, but hard, brotherly punch found its mark on Seth's shoulder.

"Dude, I'm on crutches."

"Yeah. In more ways than one." A challenging gaze pinned him.

Like looking into a mirror. Seth had given the same look to Cam when he'd caught him smoking weed behind one of their parents' stores in high school. But that butt-kicking had been called for.

"Back off." Seth's jaw tightened as anger and grief spewed out. "You don't get it. You can't. Evie's a beautiful, healthy little girl, and you've got Jonathan. While Noah..." His voice cracked.

That didn't come out as he'd intended.

Cam's stance softened. "I know you suffered an unbearable loss." He shook his head. "But you're my big brother who always had a strong faith, who has always been brave, always stood his ground against a bully no matter what size or how mean." Cam rubbed the place where he'd just struck Seth. "I love you, and I want you to see that there's a bully after you now. An evil one. He's got you on the run with his lies, but I've got your back. The whole family does. And more than that, God's got your back. You've got to stand firm, call him out, and live. You were meant for more than this."

The words slammed harder than any punch could ever land. Was that what he'd been doing here? Running from the devil? "Maybe you have a point. I'll pray about it."

"We can pray together. Now." Cam's hand still rested on Seth's shoulder.

"Okay, you first." They both chuckled at the old joke when the brothers had ever dared each other to do anything precarious.

"I got you covered." Cam closed his eyes, and they poured out their hearts before the throne.

~ ~ ~

All night, Grace thrashed between the designer sheets until she finally got up, wrapped a blanket around her shoulders, and walked out on the deck.

God, I need your help.

Her emotions crashed like violent waves in a storm, but

the words Darlene had spoken swirled within the winds. Despite disappointment over being childless, God had filled their lives with *blessing upon blessing.*

Stars, shimmering and white, dotted the darkened sky. A sliver of moon glowed, its reflection a beacon on the Gulf. An old Bible story about Abraham came to mind. He'd been promised a baby, despite the fact he and his wife Sarah were way too old to have one. Then he was asked to have the faith to be willing to sacrifice that miracle child. God saw his faith and intervened. The Lord had promised to bless Abraham and make his descendants as numerous as the stars in the sky and as the sand on the seashore. And from what she'd learned in Bible study, all who had faith in the Lord were actually considered Abraham's descendants.

A shooting star blazed a path through the atmosphere then disappeared. Grace's breath caught. "Amazing, God."

What if she took all her expectations and intentions and obsessions for her life and placed them at God's feet? What if she took one day at a time?

Maybe she didn't have to have children. After all, she wasn't guaranteed tomorrow, much less fertility and health and love. Those things were precious, but love was the most precious of all. And out here, just her and her God, staring at His beautiful creation, she had to face the truth. Though they'd only known each other a few weeks, what she felt for Seth was love.

Chapter 18

The knock on the door took Seth by surprise, especially since his *entire* family already seemed to fill every inch of his house. Man, they must've gotten up at the crack of dawn to make it by lunchtime. Good thing they brought coolers of food, because though Grace had stocked the refrigerator, the Gibbs brothers could put away some grub.

He leaned on one crutch to open the door. Grace stood there, a red sweater highlighting the blush on her freckled cheeks. So pretty, his heart sprinted, and his brain filled with fog. All night he'd wrestled with the words he wanted to say to her, brave words that might set things right if she'd accept them.

"I brought you something." She held out a green gift bag stuffed with white tissue paper.

"Grace, I don't have anything except the stuff in the garage. You can have—"

"Uh-uh. Just open the gift." She met his gaze, pleading in her eyes.

He hobbled out and shut the door. No need for a family audience. Bracing on his crutches, he accepted the gift and removed the paper.

"I'll hold stuff for you." Grace took the wad and smiled, hopeful—and adorable as always.

He forced his gaze away from her and into the bag. "What in the world?" Was this a joke? He pulled out a faucet handle, a chain from inside a toilet bowl, a sand dollar, some sea shells, and that one piece of sea glass she'd found. "I don't understand." He looked into her deep blue gaze.

"Seth Gibbs, I'm Grace Logan. I fall down a lot. I've been hurt. And like you, I've acquired a great deal of random junk in this life. Some are pretty pieces and some are just plain old broken mess." She stepped close and cupped his cheek, stealing his breath with her touch. "The thing is, you know how to fix things and how to make something special out of what others discard. God does that, too, with people. I got to thinking, maybe He could do that with us."

She was so close now, her minty breath tickled his cheek. Her fingers moved to toy with the hair along his temple. "What if we gave ourselves a chance to be there to help the other up when we fall?"

He caressed her chin. Hadn't he been praying about her all night? "What are you looking for in a man?"

"A Christian." She took his fingers and brushed her lips over them. "Calloused hands of a man who works. Good to my family. Oh..." She raised a teasing brow. "No jewelry. I'm not a fan of man necklaces, rings, and such. That's non-negotiable."

"Noted." He laughed. "I'll donate my gold chain to charity. That's a short list." Sobering, he stared into those navy blues. "I'll try to get over my issues, but like you said, I've got a lot of broken pieces. Are you sure?"

"I'm sure I can't let you go." She draped her arms around his neck. "We don't know what the future holds, only God does, but I want you in mine." Her teeth caught her lip for a moment. "Unless you don't feel the same about me?"

"Grace, I've been falling for you since that first day on the beach. More than falling—sinking into the deep. I'm crazy about you."

108

The door swung open behind him.

"Finally." Cam's voice.

"Thank you, God." Misty giggled.

"Is that your girlfriend, Uncle Seth?" a little voice chimed in.

He turned to look over his shoulder. "Y'all are teaching my niece to eavesdrop?"

Misty stepped out with Jonathan slung over her shoulder. "Come join us for Christmas Eve food and some fierce card games."

"I'd love to." Grace's smile soothed the broken places in Seth's heart.

"Merry Christmas, Grace." Seth caught her hand, weaving his fingers through hers. "My girlfriend, if you'll put up with me."

Epilogue

"Just one more box for tonight." Grace stumbled forward into the living room, but strong arms captured and steadied her. Those sturdy, calloused hands gently squeezed her forearms. She never grew tired of seeing that gold band on his ring finger, or her own silver band that held together two pearls and a diamond. The memory of his proposal on the legislature floor was one she cherished. She could still visualize him on one knee as he held out a small oval box covered with seashells.

"Grace, your bright smile and sweetness blasted into my darkness. You've shown me how to live again. Will you build something new with me? Will you be my wife?"

Of course, she'd said yes. And neither one of them took their vows for granted.

"Let me take that." Seth pressed a warm kiss to Grace's forehead. "You shouldn't be carrying a load."

Heart overflowing with love, she smiled into those amazing blue eyes. "It's not heavy. And this has to be the right container." She and Seth carried on a silent little contest to see who was the most organized. "Yes, labeled Family Ornaments and color coded with the yellow tape."

"Okay, but I don't want you worn out before everyone arrives tomorrow. You've already been cooking up a storm." He took the box and grinned. "Not that I minded that batch of oatmeal cookies, but your husband's going to end up with a Santa belly."

"The cookies were for the kids, and they were made with

all healthy ingredients. And I don't mind a dad bod. I've got the mommy one." She glanced down at her swollen midsection and ran her fingers across the little shelf where those nighttime kicks continued to bounce. "I think all the holiday events we've attended for Gibbs Hardware have worn us out. That and little Seth junior, the soccer player."

Seth set the box on the coffee table. "He's at it again?" Brows raising, he placed his hand on Grace's stomach.

Her tummy jumped beneath her shirt, and Seth gasped. "That was a hard one, buddy." His gaze met hers, tears glistening.

Grace pulled him into a hug, hoping to soothe his lingering worries. "Heather's over a year old now, and she's healthy. We can use an apnea monitor again."

"I know all that in here." He pointed to his temple. "And God's got us covered. Sometimes, the worries still creep in, especially with this one being a boy, you know. After two years in the SIDS support group, mountains of prayers, and a healthy baby girl, you'd think I'd relax, right?"

The past couple of years together in Atlanta had been incredible. Seth's foot had healed well enough, no pins and rods. They'd walked at Piedmont Park and hiked Kennesaw Mountain, married in Santa Rosa with a small, intimate ceremony on the beach, and started a family of their own sooner than planned or expected. Attending a SIDS support group had allowed Seth to process his guilt and fear, and they'd both gotten help shuffling through insecurities left from their past marriages. God had certainly moved in their lives.

Grace cupped his cheeks, cradling his dimpled jaw. "You've come a long way. We both have with God's help."

His lips quirked into a wry smile that still squeezed Grace's heart every single time. "I had you to show me how to get up

111

and dust myself off when I fall."

"And I had you to put my broken pieces back together. But in a new way." Releasing him, she turned her attention to the container. "Speaking of, let's hang our favorites." She lifted the lid and removed the layer of bubble wrap from the top row.

Noah and Heather's ornaments smiled up at them beside intricate creations of shells, sea glass, and metal. Seth had made the treasures himself.

"Would you help me finish the tree?" With delicate moves, she lifted Noah's ornament first. Seth's blue eyes sparkled in the twinkling white lights of the Christmas tree, and he touched a calloused finger softly to her lips. "I'd love to finish anything with you, Grace."

Don't miss the next book by
Janet W. Ferguson.

The Art of Rivers

A Coastal Hearts Novel
Set in St. Simons, Georgia

Chapter 1

Love, like art, took on different forms with each creator. Rivers
Sullivan quickened her pace to a skip, her ruffled skirt
bouncing in the muggy Memphis breeze. People rushed down
the city sidewalks, and cars raced by, but her thoughts rolled
with wonder over the joy in her life. Her eyes captured the way
the sun lowered on the western horizon, creating long
shadows, the way wispy clouds layered below the indigo sky.
She couldn't seem to stop herself from mixing colors and
feelings in her mind, making pictures from all she saw.

Sometimes love blurred, the shades and thin lines
smudging like the dark blues and greens and purples of a
bruise. Undefined. Her mother's love had been that way—

before the accident.

Other times, love's colors shone clear and crisp like a beacon in the darkness, bright and steadfast. Her father's love had always been strong and true, a light leading her home. Both her earthly father and her heavenly Father's love had held her on course.

Then there was Jordan. His love burst with yellows and reds, excitement and delight, exploded with gentle blues of sincerity and commitment, a feeling she'd never expected to find. Jordan had been a lifeline thrown to a lonely girl drowning in a sea of men with no conviction.

But today, love was paperwork, lovely black-and-white paperwork that would soon bond her to the man she'd never imagined existed. A man strong in his faith, his sobriety, and his willingness to wait.

And the wait wouldn't last much longer. Her face heated with the thought. Ten days. Just wearing the sparkling engagement ring still made her finger tingle after two months. She glanced at her hand, which was dotted with paint. She'd missed a few spots.

But her breath stalled at the sight of the ring.

Oh no. The diamond was missing.

She spun, retraced her steps along the sidewalk back to her Volkswagen bug, unlocked the doors, and ran her hands across the stained seats and carpet. Her head knocked the steering wheel, but she ignored the bump. In the back of the car, she lifted the canvases and paint containers lining every inch of space. *Please let it be here.*

Her fingers stretched under the seats, searching for something—anything solid. "Come on. I can't have lost it already." Maybe the stone had fallen out in the museum while she was at work. She'd never find it there.

114

Then her index finger rolled across a small, hard lump. She pinched the pebble-like matter and pulled it out from under the seat. "Let it be. Let it be."

The diamond emerged in her fingers. Her neck and shoulders relaxed. "Thank you, Lord."

After removing the ring, she placed both pieces into the front glove box for safekeeping. His grandmother's ring had fit perfectly, but she and Jordan hadn't thought to check the prongs to make sure the setting was still secure. At least she'd found the diamond. She breathed a sigh and stood up straight. A jeweler would fix the ring. Nothing could steal the joy she felt today.

"Hello?" Jordan's voice warmed her ear, his breath tickling her cheek. His hands rested on her shoulders, and he leaned closer. "You're not changing your mind about me, are you?"

Rivers whirled, her heart racing. His voice did that same thing in her chest every single time. She slipped her arms around his neck. This gorgeous man standing in front of her had to be kidding. "Never. You're my heart."

She gazed into those astounding rich brown eyes, which flawlessly matched his short dark hair. How did such perfection exist? As an artist, she'd studied colors and textures all her life, and she'd never seen such faultless coordination. Not to mention the cute angle of his nose, the dimples pressed in the center of his cheeks, and the contoured lips, which left a small shadow above his chin. She brushed a kiss across his mouth, sending butterflies to flight inside her. Still. After six months and a whirlwind courtship, she could barely wait to be Jordan's wife.

"Whew. You had me worried when I saw you go back to your ugly green excuse for a vehicle."

"Hey, don't knock the Stink Bug. She's a good car, sort of.

115

Except for the smell. And the smallness. And the age." A smile lifted her lips. "Were you spying on me again?"

"Always. That's how we met, remember?"

"I'll never forget." That day at the museum when he'd followed her to the studio still made her smile.

Jordan's gaze wandered to her lips. "We should go in before I forget why we came."

"Right. We need the marriage license to be official. I almost lost the setting from the ring you gave me. I was locking it up until I can get it repaired."

"As long as you don't lose me." His hands dropped to catch her fingers. "I'll take care of it. You *will* be my lawful wife. I ran all over town to finalize adding you to my deeds, my car title, my bank account, and my will."

"Don't talk about wills. That's depressing. Let's go be happy."

Jordan bowed and kissed her right palm. "After you."

She offered a curtsy. "My Prince Charming. I knew it the first time I saw you."

Inside the courthouse, her blue nail polish glinted as Rivers signed her name across the marriage license. Her fairy tale would be a reality soon. She giggled and danced a circle around her fiancé. "Your turn, sir."

Jordan grinned and tweaked her chin. "I do love how you move. And that cute skirt you're wearing. And your blue eyes. And your crazy blond hair. And your lips." His gaze roamed her face.

Not even the presence of the clerk could still the effect this man had on her. She took a deep breath and belted out, "I love you. I love you. I—"

"Oh, man." Jordan pressed one finger over her mouth and laughed. "Not the singing. You'll have every stray alley cat in

116

Memphis gathering outside."

The woman behind the counter cleared her throat and chuckled. "I'm still here."

"Right. Paperwork." Grinning, Jordan stepped to the laminate counter to sign his name. *Jordan Alexander Barlow III.*

And she would be Mrs. Jordan Alexander Barlow. How sweet was that?

Once they'd finished, she followed him out of the downtown Memphis government office and onto the sidewalk. The fierce heatwave that had shrouded the city for a week swarmed them. Late September meant the beginning of fall in some parts of the world, but not here. At least they'd waited until the end of the workday instead of the blistering lunch hour to get the license.

Near the car, Jordan's hand slipped to the small of her back and nudged her around to face him. "Picnic in the park? I picked up your favorite barbeque and sweet tea, and put a new sketch pad in my car."

What were the odds that she would find a man who loved her enough to know all her favorites and give them to her every chance he got? "I don't deserve to be so happy." His smoldering gaze did all kinds of crazy things to her brain. Breathing deeply beside his ear, she whispered, "Yes, we'd best move along."

"Right. Wait here, and I'll get everything." His shaky exhale made her smile. At least he felt the same. Jordan unlocked the passenger door of his Mercedes and gathered their picnic basket, sketch pad, and a new pack of her favorite pencils.

He'd thought of everything. "Thank you." She tucked the pad under one arm and the pencils into her handbag, leaving the food for him to carry.

Hand in hand, they walked toward the Mississippi. She'd

painted the mighty river hundreds of times, from hundreds of viewpoints, during hundreds of sunrises and sunsets, but none moved her like the portrait she would present Jordan on their wedding day. She'd drawn him standing there, watching her work in the early morning, golden light frolicking on his coffee-colored curls and glittering in the deep pools and currents of his gaze.

"Tell me where we're going on our honeymoon. Please." Rivers squeezed his hand, made puppy-dog eyes, and batted her lashes. "I don't know what clothes to bring."

Mischief danced in his gaze. "Just bring yourself. Nothing else required." His voice held a smile.

Heat seared her cheeks and churned up a laugh. "You. Come here." She stopped, draped an arm around his neck, and planted another kiss on his lips. All her life, she'd prayed and waited for this man. She hung there for a moment, staring. Could she ask the other question again without upsetting the perfect moment? "Did you call Jay?"

A sigh worked its way through Jordan's lips. "Tonight. I'm calling him tonight. I got his number from my step-uncle."

"Really? You're asking him to the wedding?"

His gaze dropped as he shook his head. "I can't do that to Mom and Dad."

"I would never want to upset your mom and dad. Brooklyn has been so wonderful to help plan the wedding."

"But you're right. I need to let him know I've forgiven him, leave the past in the past. Start a new kind of relationship with him." His chin rested on her forehead. "You make me a better man."

His stomach rumbled, and she pulled away.

"Or a hungry man." She smiled up at him.

"I worked through lunch again so maybe the office will

leave us alone during our honeymoon."

"They'd better. Vast River Architecture cannot have you that week. You're all mine." They passed under a cluster of trees and shrubs, and movement caught her attention. "Did you see that?"

"What?" Jordan glanced back and forth.

A shiver crept across her shoulders. Homeless people and addicts tottered around downtown areas in most cities, and Memphis was no exception. Despite the fact that she'd been in this spot often, she stopped and scanned the scene again. Something in her spirit warned of danger. "There's someone behind those bushes. Maybe in a hoodie…"

Jordan took a step and craned his neck. "I don't see—"

An explosion like fireworks popped and rung in her ears. Another blast, this with impact, hard and swift as a kick in the chest. A red-hot burning sensation pierced her shoulder and back. Time slowed, and a scream ripped from her throat.

Jordan dropped to his knees clutching his chest. Red spread around his fingers, contrasting sharply against his pale blue shirt.

Hot liquid poured all around her, and her vision tunneled white. A fountain of blood. But she had to get to him. "Jordan…" She stumbled forward and fell to her knees beside him, clutched his face. Spots danced in front of her eyes as the throbbing in her shoulder pulsed. Then darkness dragged her into its abyss.

Chapter 2

Rivers gripped the steering wheel tighter. For a brief moment, the beach views, the moss-covered trees, the beauty of this seaside town almost drowned the pain still screaming in her heart, tormenting her mind, stealing her sleep.

Almost. But black pain gathered in a huge glob on the palette of her life. Black like her insides. Void of color. Void of life. Void of capacity to feel joy.

Jordan should be at her side. He should be leading her around the town, telling stories of his childhood. The good ones, anyway. He should not be six feet under a slab in a Memphis cemetery. A memory flashed before her eyes—so much red—unearthing fresh anger, pushing the bile up her throat. One hand went to the indention in her left shoulder. Her blood ran cold and pounded in her ears. The exit wound was much larger. Too bad the shooter hadn't hit his mark and finished her.

She'd been robbed of so much more than a piece of flesh. Her heart had certainly been torn from her chest. And for what? Money to buy OxyContin or a shot of heroin? Meth? Jordan would've given his wallet, his watch...any material possession if asked for it.

The Ms. Snarky GPS signaled for her to turn. She'd nicknamed the voice Cruella, and she'd tried to obey the harsh tyrant. The seven times she'd gotten lost already on this trip had been enough, thanks to the inability to focus on anything, even the irritating voice giving directions.

The Stink Bug was doing well to make it this far. Taking the Mercedes she'd inherited would've been safer for this eleven-hour drive…okay, thirteen counting the wrong turns. But the one time she'd driven the luxury vehicle, everything in the car smelled of Jordan. She'd parked it in his drive and hadn't moved the thing since.

The roads narrowed before her. Vehicles and bright green trees crowded the streets in front of most of the houses. Jordan had always called his grandmother's place a cottage, but that had come from a man who'd known wealth his entire life, not a teacher's daughter with a disabled mother. The tints, ages, and styles of the beach homes varied wildly, as older ones had been torn down and replaced over the years.

At the end of the road that led toward the shoreline, the rude computer voice suggested that she'd reached her destination. Rivers scanned the place where the home should be. Overgrown hedges acted as a natural barrier in the front yard. No view of the cottage, no driveway yet, but the house was on a corner lot. She turned left, and there it stood.

Her pulse pounded as she slowed the car. The place looked just as she'd imagined. White cottage with a wraparound porch. Red brick chimney. Gray awnings. White picket fence around the back yard. A tattered American flag waved in the Atlantic breeze. She pulled into the short gravel drive—or maybe it was shell-lined—and parked. The fact that she'd inherited the summer home from the man who'd never become her husband shocked and overwhelmed her with fresh grief. Her parched throat dried as if it had filled with sand. She had to get out of the car, but how could she?

I don't want this, Lord. I want to forget.

This house taunted her. Reminded her of all she'd lost. The

quicker she sold everything, the better. She could get back to her clients. Her life before. If only Jordan's family had been willing to help. But they'd had their own loss that still plagued them in this town, the accident that had torn their family apart. And she couldn't ask her father. He had enough on his plate taking care of Mom. Bringing her mother would only make the task more complicated. Add too many obstacles, too many questions and frustrations. More negative emotions when she couldn't handle the ones she'd already been dealt.

It's You and me, Lord.

The heat besieged her now that she'd cut the engine, and sweat beaded on her forehead. Groaning, she opened the door and forced her feet to the ground, the mix of white rocks and shells crunching.

One moment at a time. Her pastor's words. And she knew this concept from the counseling she did for others through art therapy. Part of healing was facing the trauma. Facing the grief. *God, help me get through this moment.*

She made a path to the passenger door of her car and yanked it open. She threw her duffle over her shoulder and grabbed the pad and pencils Jordan had given her that last day. That horrific day. She stared at the tablet as though answers were locked somewhere inside the blank pages. How had it come away unscathed? That not even a drop of blood had splattered the cover seemed to be a miracle.

But not the miracle she'd begged for.

Hugging it close, she shut the door and trudged toward the front porch. The key was under a flower pot, according to the caretaker, some step-uncle of Jordan's. Kind of careless, but what did it matter? The glass French doors provided little protection, and no one in Jordan's family came here anymore. The cottage's only visitors were the folks from the cleaning and landscape services.

Up the three stairs onto the wooden planks, she stepped, then stopped. The dead plant in the terra cotta container looked about like she felt. Lifeless and withered. She bent and lifted the pot. The key lay there. She stared at the dull silver finish and imagined the pain the simple piece of metal would unlock. A wind chime tinkled from somewhere nearby, its sound melancholy and haunting.

It had taken her a year to muster the courage to make this trip. Going inside was required. Emptying the place and readying the house for sale had to be done. No one in the family had come back after Jordan's grandmother died. And as much as she wanted to forget, Rivers refused to let a stranger toss away Jordan's past.

She picked up the key, its weight much heavier than the flimsy nickel should be.

With shaking hands, she inserted it and turned. Now the knob. Already the view through the glass wrenched her heart. Pictures and paintings lined the tongue-and-groove walls tinted a whitish gray. Likely photos of Jordan and his sister, before…

Blocking out her churning thoughts, Rivers burst through and stepped inside. She tossed her bag on a nearby bench but kept her sketchpad and pencils tucked under her arm. On the opposite wall, an antique side table held five photo frames. The first one she focused on jarred her, speared through her core.

Jordan, a young, smiling teen, his sister Savannah on his back. Both tanned, they dripped saltwater where they stood at the end of a boardwalk, sand covering their bare feet and calves.

Her breathing halted, imprisoned inside her chest. She couldn't look at more. She had to get out of here.

Help me, Lord.

The chimes drifted into her thoughts again. Maybe she could draw. Outside. The beach might be the best place. With cautious steps, she glanced around, searching for where a beach towel or chair might be stored.

A set of blinders would be nice. How could she stay here with so many gut-wrenching photos? She'd have to box them up. A narrow hall opened from the living area, and a single door on the left looked to be a closet. Lips pinched and fearful of what she'd find, she cracked the door. A linen closet. Good. No pictures. A small sigh worked its way past her lips. Stacks of sheets lined the top shelf, then blankets on the next, and, on the bottom, beach towels. Beneath that shelf lay three folding sand chairs.

She snagged a red, oversized Coca-Cola towel and a fuchsia chair then made a beeline back out the door.

Don't miss the next book by Janet W. Ferguson.

The Art of Rivers
A Coastal Hearts Novel
Set in St. Simons, Georgia

Be the first to know about the release. Sign up for her newsletter.
http://www.janetfergusonauthor.com/under-the-southern-sun

Have you read the Southern Hearts Series by Janet W. Ferguson?

Did you enjoy this book? I hope so!
Would you take a quick minute to leave a review online? It doesn't have to be long. Just a sentence or two telling what you liked about the book.

I love to hear from readers! You can connect with me on Facebook, Twitter, Pinterest, the contact page on my website, or subscribe to my newsletter "Under the Southern Sun" for exclusive book news and giveaways.

https://www.facebook.com/Janet.Ferguson.author
http://www.janetfergusonauthor.com/under-the-southern-sun
https://www.pinterest.com/janetwferguson/
https://twitter.com/JanetwFerguson

About the Author

Faith, Humor, Romance
Southern Style

Janet W. Ferguson grew up in Mississippi and received a degree in Banking and Finance from the University of Mississippi. She has served as a children's minister and a church youth volunteer. An avid reader, she worked as a librarian at a large public high school. She writes humorous inspirational fiction for people with real lives and real problems. Janet and her husband have two grown children, one really smart dog, and a few cats that allow them to share the space.

Publisher's Note: This book is a work of fiction. Names, characters, any resemblance to persons, living or dead, or events is purely coincidental. The characters and incidents are the product of the author's imagination and used fictitiously. Locales and public names are sometimes used for atmospheric purposes.

Santa Rosa, Florida, is a real town, but other than the name, the events in the location are fictional. None of the events are based on actual people. The charming city made the perfect backdrop for my novel.

Scripture quotations marked (NIV) are taken from the Holy Bible, New International Version®, NIV®. Copyright © 1973, 1978, 1984, 2011 by Biblica, Inc.™ Used by permission of Zondervan. All rights reserved worldwide. www.zondervan.com The "NIV" and "New International Version" are trademarks registered in the United States Patent and Trademark Office by Biblica, Inc.™